Elizabeth LAPTHORNE

Bonded
FOR
ETERNITY

ELLORA'S CAVE
ROMANTICA PUBLISHING

What the critics are saying...

&

5 Stars "This is a wanton tale of two people who were made just for each other. I couldn't get enough of Gregor and Lani. They set the pages of this book on fire. An extra bonus was the secondary characters Leif and Sarha. If your looking for a story that will make your blood boil and drag out your own passion, go to Ellora's Cave and buy this book!" ~ *Enchanted in Romance*

4 Stars "Ms. Lapthorne has always weaved a wonderful storyline to this reviewer's eyes and feels this is truly one of her best works to date!! *Bonded for Eternity* is a decadent delight for the reader to enjoy... Ms. Lapthorne writes a wonderful book that is surely to be read over and over again! The author really lets her imagination fly in this sequel book and its definitely a prize worth having." ~ *Love Romances*

4 Stars "Ms. Lapthorne creates a wonderful background with a futuristic planet, sexy men, and Amazon women. Thereafter, taking a deceitful plot and weaving in wild and erotic sex, she completes the story for an entertaining read. This one is definitely going on my keeper shelf." ~ *Coffee Cup Romance*

"I was captivated by the description of the murals on the walls of Gregor's home. Elizabeth Lapthorne uses such flair to describe the mural so that you can easily imagine it in your mind's eye." ~ *Romance Junkies, Blue Ribbon Review*

5 Stars "Ms. Lapthorne has a gift for writing love scenes. Keep the ice handy while reading this book! It is hot. I am looking forward to reading more of this author's books." ~ *eCataromance*

An Ellora's Cave Romantica Publication

www.ellorascave.com

Bonded for Eternity

ISBN 9781419953897
ALL RIGHTS RESERVED.
Bonded for Eternity Copyright © 2005 Elizabeth Lapthorne
Edited by Martha Punches
Cover art by Syneca

This Book Printed in the U.S.A. by Jasmine-Jade Enterprises, LLC.

Electronic book Publication August 2005
Trade paperback Publication May 2007

Excerpt from *Tailspin* Copyright © Denise Rosetti 2007
Excerpt from *Spirits Shared* Copyright © Jory Strong 2007

Content Advisory:

S – ENSUOUS
E – ROTIC
X – TREME

Ellora's Cave Publishing offers three levels of Romantica™ reading entertainment: S (S-ensuous), E (E-rotic), and X (X-treme).

The following material contains graphic sexual content meant for mature readers. This story has been rated E–rotic.

S-*ensuous* love scenes are explicit and leave nothing to the imagination.

E-*rotic* love scenes are explicit, leave nothing to the imagination, and are high in volume per the overall word count. E-rated titles might contain material that some readers find objectionable—in other words, almost anything goes, sexually. E-rated titles are the most graphic titles we carry in terms of both sexual language and descriptiveness in these works of literature.

X-*treme* titles differ from E-rated titles only in plot premise and storyline execution. Stories designated with the letter X tend to contain difficult or controversial subject matter not for the faint of heart.

Also by Elizabeth Lapthorne

ॐ

About the Author

ю

Elizabeth Lapthorne is an Aussie girl, born, bred and living in Melbourne, Victoria. She graduated with a Bachelor of Science from Melbourne University and wrote her first story while looking for a job. Two and a half years later, with a Research position in a lovely company and seven published works, Elizabeth is still slightly dazed at how everything fell into place.

She had written a well-received series about the Rutledge Werewolves, and is often amused at fans/reviewers commenting on how "popular" her series is. Very recently she started to tell people about her writing career and even confessed to her parents (though she did chicken out with the explanation of what "Romantica" is). She still finds it incredibly strange to be able to order paperbacks written by herself, and is shaking with nerves at what the hell she'll write when finally asked for her first autograph.

Elizabeth is completely addicted to Tim Tams and chocolate, and barely ever goes a day without one or the other. She loves email, is a self confessed bookaholic, and has been known to buy books instead of food for herself, much to the teasing of her brothers and good friends.

She was astonished recently to be asked to do an interview…and spent a long time chewing over her responses. She loves people and adores going out for a girl's night for nachos and margaritas (unless she's designated driver, and then she eats chocolate mousse for dessert instead).

Elizabeth welcomes comments from readers. You can find her website and email address on her author bio page at www.ellorascave.com.

BONDED FOR ETERNITY

ഇ

Prologue
Planet Xylone

৪১

Leif Bardobos impatiently swiped yet *another* large frond away from his face as he made his way through the thick jungle. He grimaced and silently admitted to himself maybe it hadn't been the brightest idea to come Explore this planet with his folks. He had been so certain it would be the manly, daring adventure he had dreamed about for years. Life in New Australia, a colony created from descendants from the old world country of Australia, had become very boring.

Instead he seemed to be finding the steamy weather muggy and uncomfortable, the bugs that seemed to rule the jungle were irritating and worst of all, each tree and plant looked so boringly similar he could hardly distinguish between them all.

He had been begging both his parents, well-renowned Explorers in their own rights, for the last two years to come with them on their Expedition trips. Finally, now that he had passed into his eighteenth year and was legally considered an adult in every sense across the entire Galaxy, his parents had allowed him to travel this once with them as his coming-of-age gift.

Leif had been certain destiny had lent a hand into his affairs. Not only did he feel as eager as anything to get some decent, *real* Adventuring experience before he joined the local Guild's unit for official training, but he had *desperately* wanted to avoid his mates and their endless needling after his disastrous, and extremely public, breakup with Arcadia.

Both he and his ex-infatuation, he *could not* declare her to be his greatest-ever love *now*, proclaimed to be the one to dump the other. He insisted she had gone to dinner with Robjer, thus cheating on him and forcing him to call a halt to their relationship. She insisted he had been out one night, dancing with Helena, which he knew, of course, was utter nonsense.

He had gone out one night with a few mates to shoot a few games of virtual pool and to relax with a couple of drinks at the local bar. Arcadia had insisted she was feeling sick and not up to a night out with him. So it had been an utter surprise to see her sitting with Robjer in a darkened corner of one of the booths on his way out to take a slash in the men's room.

Stupidly, he had initiated a fight there and then. He could now freely admit to himself he had utterly overreacted, yet his masculine pride had been totally wiped out from her perceived "cheating". Arcadia had shrieked at him, said it was all *his* fault as he had been dirty-dancing with Helena the weekend before at her Majority Eighteenth celebration.

Unfortunately for him, his mates had decided with the fair Arcadia up now as *fair game*, they had to support her story and tease the hell out of him. It didn't help that neither he nor Arcadia could refute the other's story too vehemently, as they had actually broken up the following evening by a mere comm call, both of them feeling somewhat guilty.

Leif, now much more coolheaded, knew he had overreacted to a fairly simple dinner out, and secretly to himself, he had to admit he'd had one drink too many at Helena's party and might have gone overboard with his dancing.

The much-anticipated "blazing row" all their friends had been laying bets on had actually turned out to be a fairly civil conversation where both he and Arcadia had decided to break up with no hard feelings on either side.

So now while he was certainly no social pariah, a bit of out-time for all the dust to settle had been needed. When his parents had informed him of their planned Exploration he had wheedled and bargained, and finally pulled the Majority

Eighteenth coming-of-age gift plea, and had been allowed to come along. He had considered it an absolute goddess-send.

Leif shrugged and pushed the whole situation out of his mind.

Instead, he tried to focus on how a simple walk could have made him lose his direction. He was not lost, he insisted to himself. He merely didn't know precisely where he stood at this particular point in time. He continued in what he felt certain was the right direction, pushing more and more fronds away from his face as the foliage grew denser.

As the jungle he strode through became even more densely populated with flora, and not thinner as he had hoped, he swore to himself. Trying to stem the rising irritation and worry inside him, Leif silently promised to the goddess he would next time remember to carry his starmap and magnocompass with him every second until he landed back home.

Trying to bargain with her in his mind, he insisted he would place them on his person the instant he returned to the campsite and then never move without them again. Leif stopped to catch his breath, took a good look around and tried to scout where *exactly* he seemed to be in this stupid rain forest.

Leif tried hard not to growl with frustration. Coming off-planet with his folks had seemed the perfect solution to *all* of his problems. He would go away and do something *really* cool to brag about to his mates when he got back.

It had seemed in those bright moments he had first conceived the idea as if his plan was utterly faultless, as he could simultaneously gain some experience with the Adventuring he wanted to spend his lifetime doing. The Guilds always favored those who had some experience, especially from Explorer parents.

Only now he couldn't tell exactly where he was. All these damn trees, fronds, shrubs and hills all looked the same to him.

Obviously Dany and Marth Bardobos had sheltered him, their only child, from the very few less pleasant aspects of their work. They only ever regaled him with the excitement of having their research prove true and accurate, of the thrill Exploring could be. Here in the middle of a very same-looking forest Leif could hardly understand why he had wanted to Adventure at all.

Even with his parents' cautions of the rougher side of Exploring and the more detailed study and verifications needed, he had decided as a bare youth to become an Adventurer. To his eager young masculine brain, while Explorers were still cool, ninety percent of their work only required decent research skills and being able to find obscure references in the library.

Many Explorers studied their vids of the ancient papers, made their conclusions, and handed the whole lot over to the Adventurers. His parents were different in that often their initial confirmations they carried out off-planet themselves. This one case proved to be a perfect example. A rare, self-mutilating forest mouse had captured their attention here on Xylone.

Leif frowned. From his studies at school he could tell from the position in which the three suns were circled around each other very soon dusk would settle, and he really needed to be back at their camp soon.

Enlarging his steps, Leif finally swiped away a few more fronds and reached the top of the hill he had been climbing to get his bearings.

He doubted at this point his folks would be too concerned over his absence so far, but if he didn't return by dark they *would* begin to worry and that opened a whole new can of worms he wanted nothing to do with.

No one liked the results gleaned from worried parents. They tended to include stupid groundings, severe lectures and lots of ranting, no matter how old he was.

Leif also had a sneaky suspicion even though he was legally an adult now and fully able to take care of himself, whether lost or not, his mother would still vent her frustrations at him and attempt to ground him until he set off under the Guild's training. As much of this expedition was, to him at least, a face-saving mechanism, coming home grounded in no way fit into his plans.

Standing on a nearby rock formation, Leif breathed a huge sigh of relief he hadn't even realized had been caught in his chest. Just as his mind had firmed its resolve, as he *knew* he had to get his ass into gear and find his way, much of the jungle almost opened up and spread before his gaze.

Finally able to get a clear view of the surrounding area, Leif found the small curl of smoke from his parents' fire, and smiled for the first time in what seriously had begun to feel like forever.

This wasn't so bad after all!

Pulling his cap down low over his eyes in case some nasty foliage decided to whack him in the face again, Leif turned in the direction of his parents' camp and set off at a run.

He felt as if his whole galaxy had righted itself again. Instead of trudging his way up a hill, annoyed and grumpy, he knew exactly in which direction he needed to head. This spurred him on and made his feet and whole body seem so much lighter than before. He enjoyed the workout the run gave him, making him feel far more in control than he had so far today.

He laughed in delight at the utterly new sensation of freedom. For the first time in months, he began to truly understand how large and wonderful the adult galaxy out there was. How vast and brilliant it could be.

Almost making a game out of ducking the fronds, weaving between the trees, shrubs and surrounding vegetation, Leif jogged down the hill and then followed the nonexistent path back to his parents' camp.

The wind felt refreshing and reviving, rushing past him as he agilely moved his body to a tune only he could hear. The heavy *thud, thud* of his shoes echoed in his mind as they hit the soft soil, almost bouncing in his newly refound *joie de vivre*.

Leif enjoyed the feeling of being wild and free and he knew deep in his heart this was where he longed to be, out in the wild, Exploring and Adventuring. There were millions of places in the galaxy needing documentation, and he loved the sense of freedom travel gave him.

Even more importantly, he now understood some of the inhibition his father had tried to warn and instill in him. He had been warned numerous times of how easy a situation could get out of control and now Leif had firsthand knowledge of that. Yet still he could revel and enjoy those times where everything simply clicked into place.

He couldn't wait to tell his father!

Now that he had a firm bearing on where he was headed, Leif unleashed his joy and excitement. He let his own, personal self-discovery wash over him and overwhelm him.

He crashed through the trees and plants, recognizing the tiny path now in front of him leading to where his parents had set their camp.

"Hey *Muumm*," he called out as he ran up the path, "I'm not too late for dinner, am I? Dad! You won't believe—" Leif dimly sensed his feet stumble to a halt as the carnage before his eyes began to register.

At least half a dozen fully grown women, all of them around six-foot tall, stood with spears and beamers pointed toward one man whom Leif had never set eyes on before.

He and his parents had come alone into this wilderness, so for what seemed like an eternity Leif's mind seemed to

16

blank out at his non-register of this strange male. Leif's own frame had only recently grown to one inch past six foot, and so the shock of seeing the unkempt and unknown male at his parents' campsite had thrust his brain into numbed incomprehension. His mind seemingly unable to understand what it could see, it took him a moment to truly realize how unusually tall these women were.

His brain slowly trying to assimilate everything he saw, Leif stared back at the amazing women. They all wore skins, barely covering themselves decently. Yet even with the uncovered womanly flesh surrounding him he found it hard to focus on all the extreme femaleness when he suddenly saw something that made him snap back to attention with an extremely painful *thud*.

Leif saw his mother near the fire, her throat slit, the journal she always wrote her observations in clutched in one hand. Leif didn't even notice his feet taking him toward the sprawled body of his mother, didn't really register his own cries as he rushed toward her with his hands outstretched.

"Mum!" he cried out. He didn't care when a few of the women took a step forward to stop him. His brain barely even registered when one of the women called in a commanding voice, "Let him!"

Leif kneeled in the dirt, lifting his mother into his gangly arms. He blinked away tears, determined not to show any signs of weakness. Gently, unable to even think about how his mum could obviously feel pain no more, he pulled his mother away from the fire and boiling pot of what he suspected would have been another cauldron of soup.

His mother was a fantastic cook, but in such primitive surroundings, he had come to be heartily tired of soup. Yet even this thought didn't raise anything from his consciousness. He could only cradle her in his arms and try to take in what his eyes were seeing.

As he processed the idiocy and haphazardness of his thoughts, realizing he was thinking of soup and not his

17

mother, he begin to register what some of his mates had termed "shock". Here he had been worried about being late for dinner, wandering around alone at twilight. Instead, his world had been turned upside-down.

He frowned. His mum lay in his arms, her face seeming peaceful and serene. Leif kissed her cheek, firmly locking away all his scattered emotions. He couldn't let them loose just now.

Howling, killing anger, grief, remorse, loss. Thank *heavens* he had kissed her cheek and told her he loved her as she let him go into the jungle to Explore as she and his father took more vids of the mice they were studying.

His dad!

Gently laying his mother aside, making sure she lay away from the fire, Leif stood up. He gritted his teeth, determined not to let *anyone* see the wobble in his legs.

"Where's my dad?!" he shouted to the entire group. When the man still kneeling at the women's feet, surrounded by them all, sneered at him, Leif bunched his fists and took a step forward.

"Where—?" he couldn't even finish his sentence before one of the women gently nodded her head to the tent he and his dad had erected earlier in the week.

"It's too late, boy. Rodal here already slit his throat, too."

Leif felt tears burn in his eyes and throat. Suddenly, he seemed to be so very old and so very alone. Arcadia and his mates, his home and his world, everything seemed to all tilt on one side and slide away into nothingness, until only one thought entered his mind.

"I'm *not* a boy," he said loudly, sounding even to his own ears like a defiant child, "I am eighteen and am a fully grown man."

From one of the many flaps in his Adventuring pants, as his mother so fondly called them when she had bought him three pairs before they left their home—was it really less than a week ago? — Leif pulled out the beamer rifle, trying hard to stem the flow of the thoughts it evoked.

His dad had given him the rifle on his birthday. He had stated with extreme pride and even a small tear in his eye that now, as his son was a man, legally able to do anything and make his own adult decisions, he needed a real man's weapon to protect himself.

Somehow this all seemed so fitting now, as if he were going through one of the ancient rituals into manhood.

He wore the pants his mother had smiled and teased him over. He held the hand-sized rifle his dad had given him. Modern technology being what it was, everyone knew it was the smallest of beamers you had to be wary of, much like this beamer rifle.

He knew it packed quite a punch for such a small, hand-sized object. Only men and women of legal age were allowed to own such destructive weapons.

Looking carefully from the women — were they really Amazons? He had read some amazing — Leif pulled at his wayward thoughts. His eyes fell on the sneering, dirty man.

Easily a full head shorter than all of them, Leif felt guilty for a moment for his murderous thoughts.

"Did you kill my parents?" he asked softly, calmly, wondering if he could really back down now.

Although only about five minutes had passed, Leif knew he had aged a good five years in that short time. He would never return to the young, utterly naïve, carefree man he had been. He truly had entered his manhood proper.

"You stupid little shit. You're a spineless little creep just like your — "

Leif didn't even think. He turned the beamer rifle up to its highest notch, and aimed it between the man's eyes. Rodal, the Amazon had called him.

In that one split second, Leif thought of his gentle, sweet mother. She had never raised a hand in anger, not to him or

19

any man or beast. She only had an insatiable curiosity for learning and discovering new things. She and his father had loved each other so much it had sometimes hurt his masculine pride to watch them.

As Leif raised the beamer rifle up to where he knew it would end this man's life and close the circle of murder, he saw an image of his father flash before his eyes. His dad had been strong, an utter man's man, an Adventurer and an Explorer to his last breath. The mess around camp showed that they had both put up a good fight.

Looking back to the man, Leif knew what he had to do. Not just for his parents, but so he could live with himself. He didn't feel an instant's doubt or quiver in his mind.

Thankfully for his conscience, the man, Rodal, continued to utter horrid things about his mother and father. The man truly didn't seem to believe Leif would do anything to him.

Checking with one finger that the notch on his beamer sat still on its highest reading, Leif felt a strange, never-before-known calmness enfold him as he took aim.

With barely a pause for breath, he shot the man who had cold-bloodedly killed his family. Stunned surprise crossed the man's features in that instant before his death.

Obviously he truly never expected a mere "boy" to go through with it.

Leif blinked, his grief for his parents nearly overwhelming him. He recognized an extremely small sense of satisfaction deep within himself, knowing he had brought Adventuring Justice to his parents' killer, but Leif knew he would struggle to overcome the grief of losing the only two people he could ever call true family.

So lost in his thoughts had he become, a jolt of surprise echoed through him as he felt the pressure of a hand rest gently on his shoulder.

"For so slight a person, you truly are a man. Come with us, we will hold you until your family comes to rescue you."

"Rescue?" Leif asked his voice husky with unshed tears and confusion.

As he looked at the woman, he realized she was beautiful. Long, thick golden hair fell halfway down her back. Sea-green eyes stared into his brown ones with nothing but kindness and some sense of heat.

Leif tried to ignore the slight flush of red he could feel cross his cheeks. He tried hard to ignore how his cock had embarrassingly come to attention. In her skimpy skins, which he now couldn't *help* but notice, not much was left to his imagination.

"Yes. I am Sarha. We won't hurt you, unless of course you like it and ask for it most particularly."

There was no mistaking the sexual heat and invitation in those words, or Sarha's eyes. Leif swallowed. He remembered some of the stories his father had told him, after a number of drinks on their *manly* camping trips back home many years ago.

Even though *he* had been too young at that stage to drink, his father had indulged himself, and they had bonded and shared as only a father and son could. Some of the more ribald tales his father had told him had proved true throughout the years. But always the tales of the Amazonian women had lingered in his mind, never to be confirmed or denied by his father when sober.

Leif recalled the wistfulness of the stories his father's friends had told, of how the least of a man's problems would be capture by the Amazons. They were famous for their treatment of their "spoils of war". Even though many tales simply *had* to be exaggerated, no man he had met could positively confirm or deny what was true and what was the product of overheated men's imagination.

When they had returned home from that particular outing, he had questioned his Aunt Lani about what his father had mentioned. Once he had sobered, his father had refused to discuss the Amazon women any more, other than their amazing survival skills and other non-interesting features.

Aunt Lani had laughed herself sick at his story, claiming *no* woman could pleasure a man for days and not take something for herself.

His Aunt Lani!

Lani was actually his godmother, not his true aunt, but she and his mother had been through school and most of life together. Smiling at Sarha, he pulled out his personal computer and sent a message to his aunt. Noticing what he did, Sarha, gently held his shoulder and led him into the middle of the group of women.

Only daring to send a brief message, just in case the women grew impatient or didn't really approve, Leif sent it off to his aunt in the special encryption she had taught him as a kid. They frequently commed each other, but the last few minutes had sent adrenaline through his system and he struggled to try and couch his words to be dramatic enough to get her attention, but not dramatic enough to worry her unduly.

Briefly, he wondered if he would always experience this emotional and adrenaline high he seemed to be on while Adventuring.

Mum and Dad killed, he typed out quickly. *Going with group of Amazons. Coordinates are Planet Xylone, 35 north, 22 west. Help!*

Sending the message out to his aunt, hoping and praying she would get it quickly, he moved to put the unit back in his pocket, but the gorgeous Sarha held out her hand.

"Your rescuers will find you. We just have to be sure no one you *don't* want to find you can access you through this."

Leif shrugged and handed the small device over to her. With his aunt knowing his initial coordinates he had no problems handing his unit over to the beautiful woman. Before he could start up a new conversation with the stunning young woman, he found himself surrounded by the small tribe of warriors. As one unit, they began to leave the campground.

"My parents!" he insisted, turning around to look for their bodies, not wanting to leave them behind.

Sarha patted his shoulder comfortingly. "Tonia and Marina will stay behind to bury them as befitting their station. Your parents were well known to us, they were friends with us. We take care of our own. Never fear, Leif."

Leif started, surprised. "You know who I am?"

Sarha smiled. "Tonia knew your father before he Bonded with your mother. They kept in contact. The only reason we had not killed Rodal when you returned was because we were questioning him where you were. You will stay with us until your aunt arrives, yes?"

Leif had the oddest sensation in his chest as Sarha looked seriously and sensually at him. His heart constricted and seemed to simultaneously melt, he had never experiences such an odd sensation before. His cock remained firmly at attention, *begging* for her particular attention, in fact, as Sarha smiled shyly but still with some enticement at him.

He knew if he went with them he wouldn't need to take anything with him, they would care for him and feed him. Everyone acknowledged at least that much about the Amazonian tribes and women.

Remembering some of those *other* stories his father had told him, he had to close his eyes at the immense pressure growing uncomfortable in his pants. Desperately, he tried to think of something else. If his cock swelled much more, he wouldn't be able to walk let alone hike back up that bloody hill.

Feeling the pressure ease very, very slightly, he opened his eyes once more and smiled adoringly up into the beautiful woman's unusually colored eyes. As she smiled shyly back at him, a dimple popping sexily in her cheek, Leif knew she wanted him at least as much as he wanted her.

He hadn't imagined the sexual heat and invitation in those beautiful sea-green eyes. They still shone with a shy need and very hot, very sensually serious desire.

He wished for just one moment he hadn't sent *quite* such an urgent message to his aunt. Maybe he didn't want to be "rescued" after all!

Pushing aside the hovering grief at his parents' deaths which threatened to start another cycle through his thoughts as he worried about how upset his Aunt Lani would be, Leif turned his concentration back onto the dirty man, Rodal.

He felt a small amount of pity for the man, he was, after all, dead. Yet he genuinely could sense no deep remorse or heavy-laden guilt inside himself. He had brought the man to Adventurer justice. Out in the wilds, different rules applied to many "societies".

Out in the jungles and deserts, off the beaten track, if you killed someone, you had to accept someone would avenge their loved one and kill you in return. Despite the fact much of the known galaxy was "civilized", much of the lesser-traveled quadrants all agreed with this train of thought.

Adventurers in particular were known for avenging their loved ones. And Leif now truly considered himself a man and a soon-to-be Adventurer. He had done nothing out of turn. He had simply brought his parents' murderer to justice.

For a moment, Leif wondered if it were wrong of him to *want* to fully explore his rapidly growing sexual curiosity with these women, and one in *particular*, just minutes after finding his parents' dead bodies and making his first-ever kill.

"You are fine," a brown-haired woman, tall and strongly built, just like the rest of her tribemates, nodded her agreement to something he had not caught.

"It is quite natural after seeing so much death and carnage to want to reaffirm life. No one thinks the less of you. Time enough later to think and plan. Now, you console yourself in the flesh," Sarha affirmed to him.

24

A number of the women surrounding him nodded and smiled indulgently at him. His cock tightened back from being averagely hard into absolute rock-hardness bordering on true discomfort. He had never been so turned on in all his life. Not even when his mates had bought him the escort to lap-and-body dance for him back on his birthday.

Now, surrounded by so many beauties, all gorgeous in their own way and manner, he could taste the want and need growing inside him, desperately wanting to touch and stroke, caress each lovely lady in all manner of ways.

Leif smiled and followed them into the forest, a bunch of beautiful women surrounding him, gently touching his arms and chest to lead him where they wanted him to go. Each one had sensual promise in their eyes. But Sarha...Sarha touched him the closest of all. He couldn't wait to start learning the curves of her body, above all the others.

The sensual promise in her eyes told him better than any words that while all the women surrounding him might touch and caress him, might later even bring his body pleasure and release, she above all of them wanted him and they would spend much time together exploring in a different and utterly new way for them both.

Essentially a sexual novice, a virgin in the technical sense, Leif could hardly wait to get started in this particular set of explorations. Grief still sat at the back of his mind, yet his parents had always believed in living life and enjoying Explorations of most sort.

They had never believed in wailing and bemoaning one's fate and destiny. While Leif had a hole in his heart from their loss, he also couldn't help but feel excitement at what his immediate future would bring with Sarha.

Suddenly, with his mind and body focused mostly on the delicious Sarha, but also on the other Amazonian women surrounding him, Leif didn't feel certain he wanted to be rescued at all!

25

Smiling happily, he followed the group of women as they all headed back into the steamy jungle.

Chapter One

෨

Gregor warily kept his back to the wall as he watched out the entrance to the small booth. Even though the Encryption Department's library was rarely in use this early in the day, he still felt uneasy about someone coming in and accidentally overhearing his comm.

While the higher-up Management in the Force knew he and his buddy Max ran a sideline of investigations into the more bizarre cases they came across, it didn't stop the fact from rubbing them the wrong way.

In the few months they had been working on this "business", he and Max hadn't taken on more than a half dozen cases all up. What with he being so busy at work, and Max being so busy with Kyli, there just hadn't seemed to be enough hours in the day to look into more than a few select cases.

Yet they both agreed they had at least made *some* difference across the galaxy with what little they *had* managed to do.

Both he and Max knew that the instant they crossed over the line from being annoying to Management to outright breaking the rules, they both would be pressured to back off. Then again, being pressured to back off was one of the most driving reasons behind them setting up their own firm.

Not that he, nor Max, were overly concerned with what the higher Management thought or did...it just didn't do to flaunt it in their faces. As long as they didn't step on toes or create too big a fuss, the Force was willing to turn a blind eye to their after-hours snooping.

Even so, when he had received this morning's message to comm Max about *private* business, he knew it would be something he needed to talk to his buddy about without the eager young ears of the rest of the Encryption Department listening in.

He breathed a small sigh of relief when Max's image came before him. Schooling his features to show polite interest and none of the watchfulness he knew he felt, he smiled slightly.

"Max, buddy, what's up?"

"Hey there, Gregor, you wanna go off-planet for a bit?"

Gregor shrugged, knowing he had plenty of time available if he needed it.

"If it's interesting enough, sure. Why? What's happened?"

"Seems some kid has waltzed himself into the middle of an internal war. Got captured by some splinter group of Amazon women." Max snickered and Gregor had to keep himself in check so he didn't snicker in return.

While being held hostage by *any* tribal group wasn't a walk in the park, as long as one behaved oneself, the Amazon women were the best lot by far to get nabbed by. A few weeks of sexual servitude and then—unless they *really* liked you—a safe release onto some bizarre port in the middle of bloody nowhere was the captive's fate.

Neither side was ever particularly harmed, unless sexual exhaustion could be classified as a problem.

No man in his right mind would complain. There were *much* worse fates to be had.

"Okay, this one sounds brilliant, but why the rescue? Is there a reason we think the Amazons are going to become too frisky with him?" Gregor could feel the heat begin to pool down in his pants.

Usually in a rescue situation he was the backup for Max. While certainly no wimp, out of the two of them, Max had by far the more experience with black ops, or covert means. Usually Gregor rode shotgun, but by the sound of things this time around he would be going in alone.

"The kid's parents were killed nearby where he was captured by the group. Wrong place, wrong time from what intel tells me. The kid's just entered his sexual prime from what I hear, turned eighteen a couple of months or so ago. He should have no problems with the tribe at all from what I can gather, and I seriously doubt he's in danger. Remember what it was like to be eighteen?"

Both men smiled reminiscently, remembering what it was like to want nothing but sex all day and all night long. Few men were lucky enough to have a *real* sexual odyssey at that important age. Gregor knew a part of the heated burning running down and gathering in his loins was in large part mere petty jealously of the younger man.

Any man would be green with envy to have a whole tribe of women catering to his every sexual whim, as well as simultaneously teaching you the finer aspects of sexual discipline. Even alone in the world, Gregor knew this young man was one lucky son of a bitch—no one in their right mind would want "rescuing" from such a situation!

"So we're going to *rescue* this lucky dog because no one else will?" Gregor couldn't help but put some emphasis on the word rescue. More than likely the lad would fight them tooth and nail to be *saved* from such a fate.

"He sent a missive to a godmother, an SOS of sorts when he was first captured, obviously he's now praying like fury she won't come to him. But I can't see some gray godmother coming to his rescue anyway. And yeah, I seriously doubt he'll want our help…" Gregor couldn't help but snort at this obvious conclusion. Max continued, "But we really should do something to get him back. You know how these things can turn nasty at the drop of a hat. Besides, you need to find a female to partner you."

29

Gregor, who had been mentally packing and submitting his leave forms, snapped back to attention.

"What? Why? Don't tell me after all these months of Bonded bliss you're becoming some possessive fiend?" Even though he joked, and they both knew it, he knew to tread carefully here.

Max had Bonded to Kyli a couple of months ago. Modern marriage had become an individualized contract, usually entered into until both parties created a child, or until the pair's terms were met. Once the contract had been fulfilled, the marriage was easily dissolved. The institution of marriage had only become a legal document.

Bonding, on the other hand, was a permanent merging of two souls. Only certain Priestesses were able to conduct a Bonding ceremony, and often there were many "secret" — and not very publicized — requirements the Priest or Priestess required before agreeing to perform the ceremony.

Much of the secrecy was simply the different views and values the various Priests and Priestesses required. Yet after their Bonding, neither Kyli nor Max had been very forthcoming from Gregor's polite and curious inquiries.

All he had received from them was a shared smile filled with secrets, and the comment that each Bonding was individual and a truly unique experience. Mere words, Kyli had told him saucily, would detract from the beauty of the service.

Max had sat there, with an idiotic smile on his face, which proved more than anything to Gregor that the ceremony was sexual in its nature. Other than that his best mate had just smiled and nodded, practically saying, "Yeah, what she said." Which, of course, was utterly no use to assuage his curiosity.

Gregor wondered about it every now and then, but hadn't even come close to finding a woman he wanted to Bond with to try and find out.

Bonding had become a step only a small number of people entered into, as there was no way to reverse it. The merging of your souls was a permanent, serious business.

Gregor hoped his buddy hadn't suddenly become all possessive over his Bondmate. While they had once shared a threesome between them before the Bonding, and even though he and Kyli had "dated" back in their youth, their relationship was well and truly over with no hard feelings long before the threesome.

Gregor cared about Kyli, enjoyed her companionship as a friend, but had no interest in usurping Max's position with her in any way. Max, while not overly happy, had understood this well enough for them to open business together and the three of them to remain very good, close friends.

Besides, as Gregor had pointed out when they were utterly plastered one evening, it was *Max* Kyli had bound herself to for all eternity and *Max* with whom she had merged her soul. It wasn't as if she and Gregor shared any such permanent, irrevocable ties. There would never be a reason for Max to act like a jealous jerk.

Max, possessive bastard he was, knew nothing sexual or romantic lay between them. Gregor wondered if something had happened to change his feelings.

"You know I'll need a female on this particular trip. The Amazons would insist on it. Why can't Kyli—?" he didn't even get to finish his sentence before Max had interrupted him.

"Kyli's pregnant. She's not going anywhere off-planet, with or without me."

"Ah," Gregor mused softly, a pregnant Bondmate was more than enough to bring out the obsessive, possessive nature of the most coolheaded males. Even on a good day Max couldn't be called coolheaded when it came to Kyli.

Mentally, Gregor shrugged and then remembered his manners.

31

"Congratulations, my friend. Send Kyli my love and best wishes too." Gregor smiled into the comm unit, genuinely pleased for his two best friends. "Well then, I'll have to find me a partner to help with the ship and navigation. And yes," he continued before Max could throw in his ten credits, "I'll find some willing woman. Heaven knows what sort of mood the Amazons will be in when we get there. Much more easily managed with a woman of my own on board."

Gregor tried to ignore the thrill that coursed through him. He sounded like the cavemen of millennium past. "*Find me a woman*" seemed right up there with beating his chest and carrying some virginal miss over his shoulder and back to his cave for ravishment.

How long had it been since he had really *looked* for a woman as a helpmate and companion? In fact, how long had it been since he'd looked for a woman as anything more than just a willing sexual partner?

Max's snickering brought him back to the present.

"Better find one soon, buddy, you'll need to head on out tomorrow." Without even pausing for breath, Max launched into the codes and details of where the kid had been taken.

As Gregor added the details into his personal computer comm, he let his mind run over the females he knew and trusted enough to bring to the task. He needed someone who not only had enough sense of adventure to want to travel off-world into the middle of a jungle, but also someone savvy and competent enough to liaise with the Amazon tribe.

There weren't that many women he knew who fit into *either* basket, Gregor mused wryly to himself, let alone a woman who filled both needs.

When Max paused after giving him the details, he jumped in quickly, not wanting his old mate to start up on a grilling on whom he would bring. Particularly since, if he were perfectly honest, he had no bloody idea whom he could ask.

"Thanks, buddy. Congrats again on your impending fatherhood. Give my best to Kyli. I'll comm you when I'm heading off."

Max nodded and even with the fuzzy image he could tell his buddy was trying not to howl with laughter. As he had known, Max simply couldn't resist ribbing him.

"Who you gonna take, big man?"

Gregor tried not to growl with frustration. Just because he had no clue didn't mean he should snap at his best friend.

"None of your damn business," he growled, sounding for all the world like a cranky bear. He shook his head in annoyance. He hadn't meant to let his frustration show to his friend.

With that thought, and the echoes of laughter from Max in his ear, he severed the connection and carefully looked around him as he exited the booth. Even though the conversation hadn't taken *too* long, most of the booths would very soon become occupied since one of the training classes had just entered.

The vast majority of encryption agents were male, the few scattered females either useless girly-girls who only held their jobs because their daddies had high-ranking Management positions, or a couple of masculine women who had worked their asses off to get here, and had forgotten their femininity somewhere along the way.

Gregor sighed. He knew he would have to sit and think his way through all the women of his acquaintance, knew he would have to find *someone* to come along with him on the trip.

Even though the mental picture of one particular woman jumped out at him, he couldn't afford the distraction *she* would provide for him. While it might be fun to take her along, would be *wonderful* to lose himself inside her body over and over again, he couldn't afford to take and use her like that.

Especially when he would have to see her every day after that here at work.

Nope, I could definitely do without a distraction like that.

Even though he knew how seriously wrong it would be, Gregor indulged himself for just a second. He imagined Lani in front of him dressed in a light, airy dress that fluttered seductively around her knees. Her hair, the rich color of spun gold, lay unbound to fall in curls below her shoulders and her dark green eyes flashed teasingly, taunting him.

With her every move, every purse of her luscious lips she dared him to come and take her. Even though her strength, both physical and mental, was the first thing anyone would notice about her, Gregor had always thought of her and seen her as an angel awaiting corruption. With her delicious curves, her quick, eager smile and her angelic beauty, Gregor had hungered for nights on end to be the one to show her the joy in sin.

Shoving the temptation far out of his mind, he shook his head to remove all thoughts of *her*. He headed out of the library and headed back toward his cubicle in the main encryption room.

Walking the well-known corridors, Gregor let his mind wander down the darkly tempting path he seemed to travel more and more often now. Decadent thoughts of Lani…on her knees in front of him…bound sweetly, but tightly, to his bed. Image after image seared its way across his mind as he blindly walked the halls.

Finally, just as his personal favorite image crossed his mind, Gregor snapped back to attention as he reached his cubicle. While he looked at his own console, desk and chair, in reality he focused on the scene etched so deeply into his brain it never seemed far away.

Lani's hands bound to his headboard, on her knees, her deliciously rounded ass tilted toward him as his own big hands spread her cheeks wide, in that heady moment before he penetrated her ass. He could taste the anticipation on his tongue, could smell her sweet, personal perfume as she creamed for him. When she arched her back, wriggling her ass enticingly, begging for his cock to ream her ass, he had to fall back to reality with a *thud*.

He had a raging boner and needed to sit at his desk *right now* before he invited comment from either his superiors or the many men and women who worked with him.

With an incredible effort of will, Gregor dragged his mind back to the task at hand. He wished like fury he could invite Lani along with him, yet he knew it would be incredibly stupid and dangerous. While the task of rescuing the "kid" wasn't super-urgent to his mind, more than likely he would refuse to come with Gregor anyway. He could only spare a day, two at most, before heading on out on the mission.

He sat down at his desk and switched on his work computer, smiling as the holo-screen rose to greet him as always. Entering his private account, he began to sift through the day's work.

Ten minutes later, Gregor found himself leaning back at his desk, eyes wide with equal parts amusement and sheer disbelief, job and work completely forgotten. He could barely believe the small, sexy-looking animated brown fox taunting him by blowing him kisses really sat on his holographic screen.

Decrypt me if you dare! the vixen taunted him, speaking in a purely feminine, husky, sex-laden voice.

Even though brown foxes had become extinct in the last millennium, Gregor had always been a big fan of his teenaged history classes and tutorials. Yet somehow the upright, walking, "talking" animal had become feminine and sexy. It was an anatomically correct vixen, with no boobs, no nipples and certainly no pussy to be seen, yet it easily conveyed the fact it was feminine by its posture.

Besides what his senses told him and what he could gather from its posturing, the vocal taunt was pure female.

Decrypt me if you dare, indeed! Gregor had never yet met an encryption program he couldn't unravel, and he felt absolutely certain no upstart young female would beat him yet!

Casting aside his numerous other tasks impatiently awaiting his attention, pushing the kidnapped man and tribe of Amazons awaiting him all to the back of his mind, Gregor bent over his keypad, inbuilt to the desk for his ease, and began to do one of the things he did best...un-encrypt data.

* * * * *

Lani grabbed herself just in time, before she could fall out of her chair from shock and excitement.

Yes! She imagined herself pumping her fist in the air. *Yes, yes, yes, YES!*

He was intrigued, determined to decrypt her message. Finally, after nearly three weeks of working in the cubicle across the room from the Almighty Gregor she had managed to snare his attention.

"Better watch yourself, Laynie, you don't want that pretty ass splayed all over the floor. Oh, hang on! We all do," came the sneer from the cubicle next to her. Lani sighed and gathered her wits. Reminding herself about the nasty penalties for murder, maiming and dismemberment of a fellow Force member, Lani turned to her cubicle buddy, Jym.

"Jym, darling, would you like me to stencil my name on your forehead. After three weeks of working in each other's back pockets I'd have thought you would know it by now. It's pronounced 'Lah-ni', and well you know it."

Jym clutched his chest, as if in the throes of climax, or maybe it was heart failure, she thought wishfully.

"Would you, honey? Then everyone would know how you feel about me."

Lani turned back into her holo-screen and tried not to smile. Jym might be a decryption nerd in all the ancient stereotypical ways, he might also be annoying and an utter "dork" as her grandmother had used to say, but he could make her smile when she was on the edge of despair.

For three weeks now she had been working with the International Secret Services in the Encryption Department. Three weeks of grueling work, deadlines coming out her ass, and mooning like a lovesick teenager over Gregor, their "brain man" and "secret weapon".

Despite him still not even being aware of her existence, even though she had successfully managed, in the most juvenile manner she had indulged in her entire life, to bump into him almost every day in the break room, she persevered.

Oh, the Almighty Gregor knew her name, knew where and how she had been recruited. Yet he never once had looked at her as if she was a woman, as if she were anything other than yet another male in this male-dominated environment.

When she had arrived early this morning, her inner vixen had jumped outside her mind and onto her screen, literally, and she had nearly laughed aloud at the simplicity of her plan.

First. Get Gregor's attention—not the easiest feat on the planet.

Second. Get him to meet up with her—again, no simple task.

Third. Fuck his brains out until he couldn't walk a straight line.

Lani was sincerely hoping this final task would prove easier than the previous two. She had been doodling on her holo-screen, playing and toying with images and a new encryption code she had been slowly building.

The basic premise was so simple, any child who with their own personal computer box and a rudimentary knowledge of encryptions could work it. And therein lay the secret key. Jym had spent six hours of pure frustration yesterday using every devious, nasty, low-down-and-dirty trick he knew trying to unlock her holo-screen, until she had come in on the swing shift.

Lani had been wondering if it were simply a twist of the feminine mind. Look for the simple answers, and then move on to the more complex solutions. Either way, with a few casual twists turned into the code for laughs, Lani had found and made what she truly felt certain was a practically unbreakable code.

Every Force member knew there was no such thing as a completely unbreakable code—yet Lani had enough confidence in her work she truly believed she had come as close as humanly possible to creating one.

Late last night she had commed one of her Supervisors, her only female Supervisor, Jayd, and had described the encryption program she'd made.

Jayd had been positive, but cautious, explaining that she needed a blind testing of it before she took it to the Managers. Lani had chewed over her thoughts all through the night, and had decided early this morning to use Gregor as her test subject.

There seemed a certain irony in it. Not only would it grab his attention—Lani's knees wobbled at the thought of how her code might affect him—but it would also be irrefutable, unavoidable proof for the higher Managers that her code was good, and was worth a serious look.

Of course, the imp in her mind positively *loved* the idea of how ironic her style would be, "using" the Department's secret weapon against them for herself. Besides, *anything* to do with her interaction with Gregor was brilliant to her frame of mind.

If Gregor acknowledged how clever and devious her code was, Management couldn't possibly ignore it—or her. Yet so bold a plan had made her hesitant to throw herself into it. If Gregor took it as an insult, or if he *didn't* recommend it to Management, then she was screwed. And not even literally!

It hadn't been until Gregor had merely grunted his greeting to her at the start of their shift that feminine pique had finally won out, insisting she challenge him more daringly.

Sitting in her cubicle, typing away madly, she had acted like a woman possessed, or a woman on a mission. Which she often seemed to be after her frustrating encounters with Gregor.

Toying with her graphics, she had come up with the feminine fox figure. Deciding to go for broke, she had written the most come-hither message she dared inside her code for when he finally broke it, as she was fairly confident he eventually would.

If you want to meet the special woman who made this code, meet her later tonight at the Green Island Bar at midnight. She will contact you.

Sneaking yet another glance at the studiously bent head, dark blond hair partially covering his face, silver-gray eyes intensely focused on his work, she quivered as a shiver of erotic desire flow through her. She knew Gregor well enough to know that any task he set his mind to, he dedicated one hundred and ten percent to it.

Nothing ever got past his notice, yet he could so casually ignore her and the sensual promise and electric chemistry that flowed between them every time they shared space.

Well, at least she'd know for absolute certain after she met up with him if there really was any potential between them.

Now all she had to do was wait and try to be patient. *Patient isn't something I do well*, she acknowledged to herself, tapping her fingers on her desk. Suddenly, her computer announced she had a new message, one that had been delayed a few hours due to inter-planetary static.

Inter-planetary static? Who would be contacting her from off-world?

Bringing up the odd message, grateful for the distraction, the first thing she noticed was the "Inter-planetary static" actually had been caused from the remoteness of its sending beacon. And the "few hours" were in fact nearly a whole day's worth of delay.

Frowning, wondering whom the message could be from, she opened it, her curiosity humming in excitement.

To her trained eye, an easily recognizable, code came upon her screen. The message read simply, only being a few short sentences. Lani could feel the hammering of her heart as it beat faster and faster. Even before her mind routinely began to decrypt the data, the use of the simple code gave her a good idea who the message came from.

Leif, her godson, had begged her a number of years ago to share her knowledge of encryption. His parents, Dany and Marth, were good friends of hers, and happily had shared the joy of raising their child with her. Lani and Marth had gone through schooling together and often kept in touch. Lani had been delighted to teach the then younger Leif her knowledge.

Since teaching him, it had become a running joke between them to message back and forth in codes. They always tried to challenge each other, make codes harder and trickier to break.

In truth Lani had been going to test her new code on Leif next, just to annoy the kid. The fact this code was so easily recognizable made her feel queasy. It must be something truly important if he wasn't even *trying* to stretch her mind.

Easily, within minutes, she had the message decrypted.

Mum and Dad killed. Going with group of Amazons. Coordinates are Planet Xylone, 35 north, 22 west. Help!

Jumping up from her desk, Lani began to pace the few steps of floor she had been graced with. She had no care or concern for the odd looks her colleagues gave her. She needed to go help her godson and she needed to go now!

The only problem lay in she had no ship, no means of getting to Xylone. She couldn't hire a ship, as that required crew and she couldn't afford that if she were only leading them in to be slaughtered. Who knew what sort of scenario would be waiting for her? Particularly if her old friends had been murdered!

Throwing herself back into her seat, Lani set to work. She would research as much as possible tonight, both on this tribe of Amazon women and their practices, as well as the situation on Xylone.

But what about her meeting with Gregor?

Lani gazed unseeingly at her holo-screen. She had heard rumors of Gregor and his exotic cases, how he had been to uncharted planets and back again. He would be the utterly perfect man to call to help her with rescuing her godson.

Lani smiled. It also gave her a legitimate reason to meet up with him later tonight at the rendezvous and ask for his help. Sure, she had been planning to throw herself at the man, but that would have to wait for now. Her godson came first.

Besides, she could always jump Gregor's bones later. She'd already been waiting three weeks. What was the problem with waiting a few more?

With that all worked out in her mind, Lani turned her screen back on from the holo-screen saver and set about unearthing as much data as possible. She was determined to get much research done, partially to impress Gregor, but also to give her more confidence about the unknown planet.

Lani sensed the familiar surge of power and happiness as she opened up her computer and began to hack. She'd need to sift through all the information, combining ti all so nothing would overlap, or be told twice. Research was her specialty, and soon she had settled into her routine.

She wanted to be thorough as well as informative. She needed to bowl over Gregor at their meeting when she presented her case to him at midnight.

Chapter Two
Later that night

പ

Lani closed her eyes and stretched her legs out until they both pressed against the far wall of her cleansing cubicle. While she would have much preferred to have a bathing enclosure, where she could lie down flat in the heated water, the next best thing a girl could pamper herself with was the lodging's cleansing cubicle.

She had purposely arranged for a lodging with one of the newer models installed. With an inbuilt seat of breathing leather and old-style walls, it physically looked like the showers from the old millennium. Yet a cleansing cubicle was so much more.

Heat exuded from the floor, walls and ceiling of the cubicle, yet would not burn her if her feet rested near the porous exits. It felt so completely relaxing at the end of a hard day, or night depending on her shift and duties, to sit down on the comfortable seat and let the heat and steam waft around her naked body.

Smoothing her favorite lotion onto her skin, she let herself relax, muscle by muscle. The heat and steam cleansed her far better than any regimental shower could. Lani knew she would feel even better if she could soak in a bathing enclosure.

However, the knowledge that she relaxed in her own lodging and, more importantly, had complete and utter privacy for whatever she wanted to do, made her moan in ecstasy as her head fell back to rest on the wall.

Lani closed her eyes and breathed the steam deeply into her system, imagining the heat cleansing her insides as well as her outer skin. The cleansing enclosure had long ago become

42

her special spot, her one place where she could be feminine, let herself go and indulge her body.

She had already ordered the cubicle to let the old, wildflower scent of jasmine waft through the small room. The light, flowery fragrance gently underscored the heat and rising steam that would eventually cleanse her system. For just another second Lani enjoyed the sweet, fresh scent permeating the room.

Adjusting her position so she could happily stay in the one spot for a while, she evened out her breathing. Slipping into a light meditative trance, Lani enjoyed the time and space to just let go and breathe.

For too many years she had been under constant pressure, never being able to truly relax on the long trips on the ship. Even then, with so many men on board, and so few women, she had never been able to pamper herself or indulge either in her own space or her sexuality.

With coed cleansing cubicles the few women always made sure they simply washed their bodies and then moved out. Not from fear or anything else so juvenile, but simply to prove they weren't wasting the ship's small store of supplies.

Women who indulged in anything more than her male comrades always invited trouble to themselves. With everything so strictly regimented between every person equally, if someone took more than their fair share, someone else would undoubtedly miss out. Particularly if a woman indulged, it invited censure and teasing at the least, or a reprimand from their Commander or a black mark against one's personnel record at the most.

Yet secretly, steam bathing, or true bathing, had always been one of Lani's indulgences. She continued to breathe in the steam, letting every inch of her body relax.

Without her permission, her thoughts trailed back to Gregor. Had he finished decoding the message yet? She knew in her heart he would eventually. Gregor was not the sort of man who left for home with a task incomplete. He would simply keep on decoding until he became successful.

Much as she admired the man, she knew his weaknesses as well. Pigheaded being an apt description for the stubbornness he displayed. The man simply never knew when to quit. Not that he could in this case. She had been excruciatingly careful to cover her tracks, so not knowing who sent him the missive would pique his pride as well as his curiosity. He would *have* to decode it to discover its meaning.

Despite herself, she could hear her breath coming faster at the thought of Gregor. With his deliciously hard muscles, the large width of his shoulders, the silky threads of his hair, piercingly direct gray eyes, and his long legs all combined made him one hell of a man and desired by almost every woman in the Force.

He exuded the strength of a man who had been through hard training and had come out the other side of it utterly successful. He had been out in the field for a number of years, not just sheltered here in the headquarters for his entire career. This, she knew for sure, gave him the slightly harder edge than most of his colleagues.

Moaning at the image of his naked body that played across her mind, Lani cast aside any thoughts of a relaxing meditation and spread her legs.

Luscious thoughts, images and fantasies of Gregor flitted through her mind, one after the other and could not be tamed. For once she was completely alone, in her own lodgings, in her own cleansing cubicle. She could indulge herself all night and no one would be the wiser.

Well, she mentally corrected herself, *until the prearranged time to meet Gregor, but there was still plenty of room to maneuver until then.*

Feeling giddy at the freedom, she let her index finger run along her slick outer labia. Gently moving her finger up and down, collecting the dew already weeping from her body in desire, she shifted her position, her legs braced, so she could enjoy the heat of the steam as well as her own ministrations.

Keeping her lips separated with one hand, she gently found her clit with her other, hissing in sensitivity at her rough fingertip. Collecting more cream, she lubricated her finger and moved back to her engorged clit.

Stroking over it carefully, she found her own rhythm. *Stroke, stroke, dip, stroke.*

Relaxing more as she let herself fall deeper into her own desires, Lani began to imagine, to let her fantasies run wild.

She would be in her own bed, lying naked on the sheets. The night would be warm, steamy. She would have left her windows open in the vain hope a cool breeze would come by. Her body would be faintly covered in sweat, just like she felt now. Her muscles would be lethargic but needy, her body flushed. She would roll onto her back and spread her legs.

Wide apart, like she had them now.

Lani closed her eyes and imagined leaning her head back, almost feeling the soft pillows that would lie beneath her head. As she stroked two slick fingers inside her pulsing heat she arched her back and a small moan escaped her lips. Her inside walls clamped down tightly on the two slick fingers, yet she still needed more.

Briefly, she wished for the hard, full length of Gregor to be thrusting deeply inside her. Instead she only had two of her own slim fingers teasing herself. Lani stroked herself harder, teased her inner walls until she felt a pulse of electric current run through her. She sucked in a deep breath.

She had found her G-spot. Gently, tenderly, she rubbed herself there again. Lani moaned, pressed her feet harder into the wall and spread her legs even wider to allow a deeper penetration of her fingers.

Lani increased the pressure of her other hand on her clit, built the tension inside herself. Her head tossed from one side to the other.

And then she imagined seeing Gregor climb inside her opened window. In the darkness of the evening, the darkness of her room, the man himself seemed as dark as the night, half a shadow himself. He would creep into her room and flash that handsome, devilish grin.

Lani felt her breath catch at the reality of her vision. He would lean against one corner of her room, smile that white, hungry smile, and watch her please herself.

"Don't stop on my account," he would drawl, his eyes devouring her open and stretched-to-the-limit pussy.

Lani twisted in desire as her blood heated. Everything became more real, more sensitized under his gaze. Something that had until now been secret and slightly naughty became lavish and decadent. She spread her legs wider, to give her imaginary Gregor an even better view.

Lani rubbed her clit harder, knew her climax had begin to build deeply inside her. She slipped a third slim finger inside herself and the full, heavy sensation was almost more than she could bear.

Canting her hips, she pressed herself into her own ministrations. Wanting more, wanting Gregor's cock to be pulsing inside her, and not just her own fingers, she let her moans escape her mouth. No sense in being quiet or repress her responses, since she was alone.

As she could sense herself reach further for the elusive climax, she could see Gregor in her mind, watching her. She could feel the heat of his gaze upon her body. As she stroked one slightly rough fingertip over her engorged clit, she felt her whole body seize up. She pressed her head harder against the cubicle wall as her pussy contracted around her fingers, sucking them as if nothing else mattered.

In the back of her mind, her dream-Gregor watched her every movement in thorough fascination.

"Tell me, Lani," he purred seductively at her from where he stood, "has anyone ever reamed that ass of yours?"

Lani moaned as her climax ripped through her, draining her of her strength. She had no idea where that last comment had come from. She never acknowledged, even to herself, some of her darker desires that haunted her dreams sometimes.

In her deepest heart she sometimes dreamt of being bound, or saw enticing mental or dream scenes of herself dressed in nothing but a thong and lacy bra being ordered sternly to suck a man off, or to lie across his lap for a spanking.

And in the very darkest, most secret hours of the night, tucked up in her own bed and far away from anyone else, she dreamed of bending over and wiggling her naked ass in front of a man like Gregor. She dreamed of teasing and taunting him with her submissive streak, offer to let him do anything he desired to bring her pleasure, or admit her willingness to do anything to *him* that would bring him pleasure.

He, of course, would be instantly struck with a heated desire and bend her over whatever was handy, a chair, a table, even have her on all fours on her bed. And he would prepare her ass, and then ram his hard cock inside her.

Lani had never seen or heard any indication that Gregor was interested in being a dominant man in the bedroom, yet still her dark fantasies would persist.

Like everything else in her life, she had fully researched the mechanisms and reasons behind her bondage fantasies. She knew her dream-Gregor would need to lube her ass and prepare her carefully. But one day, when the right man came along, she would let him do this to her. And she would love it.

A small alarm tinkled in the cleansing chamber.

Damn, she cursed, groping for a small hand towel, *time to get ready for the meeting with Gregor.*

Sitting upright, letting her feet fall back onto the floor, she wiped herself down. Standing slowly, Lani stepped into the adjoining shower. She quickly let the warm water run over her body as she washed away her own juices and slathered more subtly scented cleansing lotion over herself to complete the feminine ritual.

She hurriedly dried herself and rushed into her bedroom to dress for the meeting. Well-used to last-minute, important packing, she placed a couple of changes of underwear and clothes, as well as a few essentials into a small, light bag like the most seasoned of travelers. This completed, she grabbed the folder of information she had gathered earlier in the day.

Details of Xylone as well as the couple of Amazon tribes that resided there were all neatly categorized and ready for Gregor's perusal. Folder tucked firmly into the small bag, she headed out to make her meeting with the man she had fantasized about for more nights than she cared to admit to.

* * * * *

Gregor squinted in the dim light. His eyes ached and he could feel cramps in each individual finger muscles. His throat was parched and he couldn't remember the last time he had eaten.

Breakfast, his mind interjected, *before that vixen pranced over your holo-screen and brought this miserably, damnably difficult code into your pathetic life.*

Oh right, it had been breakfast.

Pushing his chair back from his desk, rubbing his eyes with aching fists, he took a few deep breaths and tried to calm his mind. For just a moment, his eyes flicked to the clock on the opposite wall. Five minutes to eleven.

Standing up, bending the cricks out of his neck and back muscles, he looked around the large office room and was vaguely startled to see he had the entire place to himself. He hazily remembered everyone else slowly fading out, carelessly thrown farewells as people headed home to their lodgings and families.

He frowned as he remembered Lani had ducked her head inside his cubicle, looking curiously at his screen as he muttered curses to the she-devil who had sent him the code.

"Heading off now," she had cheerily proclaimed. "I think three hours of overtime is enough for any girl." He had inwardly cringed at the reminder of her gender, not that he needed any help in *that* department when it came to Lani.

"Do you want me to order something in for you to eat?" she had continued, blithely unaware of the havoc she wreaked on his body and senses with her easygoing mannerisms and casual femininity.

"No. Thanks."

Gregor spent a second analyzing his response to the woman who haunted his dreams. Brief and to the point, he noted, satisfied. Not in any way rude or offensive, yet neither inviting more conversation. No sense in borrowing more trouble when his system was already overloaded from all the concentrated code work he had been doing for nearly six hours straight.

He had watched her shrug and wave again out of the corner of his eye. He could hear her leaving the room and eventually the building in the silence of the late evening. He gritted his teeth as he realized that minor exchange had left his body all hot and coiled, desperate for some action or sexual release.

More hours of diligent coding had cooled his sexual ardor, but now had left his muscles all slightly cramped. After a few more simple stretching exercises, casting all thoughts of the frustrations of the day behind him, he dropped his body back casually in his Galaxy-proved-ergonomically-correct chair. He leaned back and closed his eyes to better picture Lani.

Tall and built, were the words that came to mind. Large, beautiful breasts his palms itched to hold and weigh. Shoulder-length blonde curly hair, which always seemed tamed and not messy, no matter the time of day or night. The curls probably seemed perfect to him as they were set off by creamy white skin. He would bet serious amounts of credits she had the Irish somewhere back in her ancestry. Hot Irish.

He had never seen her blush, but knew with a male instinct she would look perfect flushing so that her pale skin and shiny golden curls would make her look like some seductive, sexy angel, just begging to be corrupted.

Never one to back down from a challenge, Gregor had jerked himself off many nights imagining making those curls messy and run wild, to see the flush of sexual need and desire flash in those wicked green eyes. One of his favorite fantasies was to muss those curls, make her cheeks and other areas of her body flush, and then command her to open that rosebud mouth of hers and suck him dry.

Goddess, I'm about to shoot my load just thinking of it!

His next favorite fantasy, of course, was to bind her to his bed, spank her lightly until her ass flushed a delicate shade of pink, and then ream her until they both screamed his lodging's walls down.

Oh yeah, he wanted her bad.

Gregor knew she was fleshy in all the right places, with enough meat on her thighs, arms and stomach for a man to hold onto. Gregor loved a woman who wasn't bone-skinny, or so heavily muscled she seemed masculine.

He liked his women to be women, and maybe that was half his problem with Lani. She was so very feminine, yet still muscled and toned enough he knew she could keep up with most men physically.

The other thing that drew him like a moth to the proverbial flame was, unlike most other women in the Industry, she was obviously self-confident—in her looks, actions as well as her skills. Like any other woman in the Force she certainly worked both her body and mind hard to make sure she was in peak condition, mentally as well as physically.

Just thinking about her like this made him hard as iron.

Knowing no one else was in the building he pulled his shirt out from his pants, untied them and let his aching shaft come free. It was thick with the strength of his arousal.

Spreading around the few drops of pre-cum already showing his readiness, down he fisted himself, moaning at the pleasure that shot though his system as he handled his long shaft. He grimaced, reluctant to admit the true level of desperation his need for Lani had created inside himself, yet the level of his lust was so powerful after only a few stray thoughts of the woman he didn't really see how he could continue to ignore it for much longer.

He really needed to do something about his obsession with her.

Must be time to go out and get laid again, buddy.

Casting all thoughts of taking another woman out of his mind, he easily pictured Lani, naked before him. Building the fantasy slowly, wanting to draw the whole scenario out, he imagined her hair, a blonde, curly, soft cloud around her face. Her long, slender neck was arched, her breasts thrust invitingly toward him.

Her legs were spread, the short, pale blonde curls gleaming with her pearly dew, begging for his tongue, his mouth upon her. Her hands stroked her outer lips, toying around her clit.

Gregor gripped himself at exactly the pressure he loved. He didn't need to heighten his own arousal, yet drawing the moment out, building the tension in himself and his fantasy made him hungrier for his fantasy woman. Running his slick palm up and down his shaft, he timed his own fisting to his mental picture of Lani stroking herself.

Groaning as he moved his hand faster, he lowered his other hand to play with his sac. He could feel the pressure mounting, growing and building inside his stomach and balls. More and more pre-cum wept out his tip, lubricating his fist and shaft as his strong grip ran up and down, building the pressure inside him. As his imaginary Lani moaned her own desire, arching her delicious breasts toward him, erect tips begging for his mouth, he moaned himself, desperate for relief.

He couldn't help the instinctive jerking of his hips, in perfect sync with the panting breaths of his fantasy-Lani. She needed him to thrust deeply inside her, needed his hot, hard length ramming itself inside her core, to sate her hunger as well as his own.

As his need grew deeper, darker, he altered the fantasy. As much as he desired to thrust balls-deep inside her, he didn't want to fantasize about that, he wanted to do it in reality. So he altered the fantasy.

He imagined Lani, hands bound gently behind her back, balanced on her knees. He could feel the heat inside his stomach turn in to a liquid molten fire. He knew himself well enough to understand the darkness inside his soul, to know that while he would *never* hurt a woman, a small amount of pain in the right place and time with a proper amount of skill behind it could bring any woman immense pleasure, no matter what her sexual preferences were.

He could see her there in his mind's eye, her hair tied back into a bouncing ponytail so her face with all its clear angles looked perfect. On her knees, face upturned he imagined her sweet, soft mouth opened wide around his thick shaft, sucking him off.

Her eyes would tilt upwards, their dark, wickedly hungry green depths looking like twin pools of lust and temptation. She would snare him and he would drown in her liquid desire.

Her mouth, opened wide around his immense cock, would be stretched to its limit as he would be as deeply down her throat as he could push himself.

As he pinched the sensitive point just under his sac, he simultaneously imagined Lani sucking him so strongly he could feel the fire gathering, about to explode. He fisted his hand around himself tighter, knowing the end of his restraint drew close. He was completely out of control, on the knife-edge of his sanity.

Finally, knowing he was about to blow his wad, he imagined lifting Lani's mouth from his shaft with one hand, and turning her around so she rested on all fours. Holding her bound wrists with one hand in his imagination, and holding her hips steady with his other hand, Gregor tightened his real fist on himself as he pictured plunging himself inside his dream-Lani from behind, right up to the balls.

He instinctively knew she would arch her back with delight as he entered her, thrusting his thick, hot shaft inside her entrance. She would cry out with the pleasure of his deep penetration, and he could feel himself begin to come, both in reality and in his fantasy.

Yet unlike his fantasy, he didn't come inside the delicious Lani, didn't let his seed shoot up inside her, bathing and warming her womb. Instead, he came all over his stomach and hand in white-hot jets of seed. His legs shook and his arms began to cramp at the tightness of his hold on himself. His mind spun with the lack of oxygen inside his system.

Panting, sweating from the intensity, both of the climax and his fantasy, Gregor leaned back in his chair, uncaring of the sweaty smell of post-sex that permeated the room and his cubicle.

Feeling as if he had just run a marathon, he gasped in deep breaths as he caught his breath. Giving himself a moment to recuperate, knowing he would need to tidy himself up as well as switch up the air circulation to get rid of the decadent smell of sex, Gregor let his gaze fall on his holo-screen.

His blissful state began to dissipate as he thought of the futility of his fantasies about Lani. Everyone knew you couldn't have a personal relationship with a member in the same division. It was one of the most basic rules of the Force, and had been in place forever.

Knowing he could never act on his fantasies only made them darker, more hot, even more decadent and forbidden. The sheer force of lust he had for Lani hadn't abated in the long three weeks they had been together in the department.

As his frustrations mounted, Gregor ran an agitated hand through his hair, mussing it further. Annoyed both at the she-devil with the seemingly unbreakable code as well as Lani, the unattainable sexual goddess, he heartily cursed women in general.

How very like a damned female to send him a damned encryption program with no warning and no hints. Only that damn vixen.

Stripping casually as he crossed the rooms, he shoved his sweaty clothes into his locker and placed his shoes as well as his clean clothes on the bench as he headed straight into the adjacent shower stalls. Thankfully, all sections of the Force held lockers and shower units. Officers never knew what hours they would keep or what sort of incidents would happen, and so large shower blocks were built in with lockers and a towel service adjacent to each main division.

Obviously Management didn't have post-coital showers in mind as the general use of the services, but Gregor had never really cared for Management anyway.

Setting the spray to its full level, wanting to wash away all thoughts, both of Lani as well as the damn vixen awaiting his return, he tested the water and then stepped into the stall. Letting the heated water pour down over his body, grateful he always kept a spare change of his suits in his locker, Gregor cleaned away the evidence of his lusts and frustrations. Squeezing a small amount of general cleanser into his palm, he ran some of it through his hair, rubbing the last of it over his chest and under his arms. As he scrubbed away his frustrations and sweaty climax, he idly pondered his problems.

The Lani problem was hopefully the easier of the two to solve. Obviously his fierce reaction to her lay in the fact it had been way too long since he had had a woman. Picking up with someone else, indulging in a day, or night, of hard sex would alleviate the severity of his need for her.

Or at least he hoped that would work.

A female, he mused. His mind instantly segued into his *other* problem.

The only clue he had to the code lay in the knowledge the programmer was a female. Women thought along different lines to men. Sometimes they were far, far more complex than any given man. Yet when it came to logic, often women were far more clear-cut and direct, far more straight-and-narrow in their thoughts.

Rejuvenated, both by the shower, his jerking off, as well as his new train of thought, Gregor dried himself impatiently and pulled his new black skinsuit on with barely a thought. He hurried out of the locker room with his damp hair still a mess around the collar. Gregor pulled on his shoes and socks, his mind concentrating on the ramifications of his thoughts. He quickened his stride as he moved toward his cubicle, his mind ticking away at a fast rate.

Typing furiously at the keyboard even as he dropped himself back into the seat, he muttered nonsense to himself as he could feel the connections snap into place at lightning speed.

Ten minutes later he sat back in both awe and frustration.

If you want to meet the special woman who made this code, meet her tonight at the Green Island Bar at midnight. She will contact you.

Reading, and then rereading the cryptic message, Gregor could feel a smile tug at his mouth. *She will contact me, huh?* Looking at his watch, he knew he would have to pack up and leave immediately to meet the assignation.

Gregor had thought briefly when the message had first arrived about tracing its source. Actually, there had been two reasons behind him not tracing it. The first was any hacker good enough to make a code he had incredible difficulty breaking would know how to make it just as difficult to trace his source.

Secondly had been his pride. He had been the best code breaker for years, had been top dog most of his life. The unwritten rules were always to break the code first, and *then* the hacker revealed himself—or herself, as the case might be. These rules might be unwritten, but always known. Besides, if the hacker hadn't made the assignation, he would have been able to trace the source and find them. He just would have been pissed when he finally caught up with them.

Knowing who sent the code and vixen might have saved him a lot of hassle and frustration, yet he wouldn't be feeling the sated pride he currently experienced. As he had invented and set up much of the software the department used, he knew intimately all the back entrances and trap-doors to use.

It would only take him a short amount of time to see where the package had originated, but that was a task for tomorrow. Saving and printing his data, he mentally took his hat off to the woman who could not only catch his attention so easily, but also had the balls to do so in such a manner.

Closing up his site, he double-checked the safety of his gear as well as how slimly he was cutting it to the deadline. Knowing he would have to speed a bit, Gregor headed out of the building at a fast pace.

Entering his Cruiser, he headed to the bar where they would meet. He might end up a few minutes late, but all in all he was nevertheless rather proud of himself for making her deadline. Most other men would still be struggling.

Truth be told, if he hadn't taken his break and jerked himself off and then been struck with his epiphany, he might still be typing away furiously.

He smiled as he realized in part he owed his success to Lani. If she hadn't blown his mind, as well as his balls, the release of tension would never have occurred.

Still smiling and thinking possessive thoughts of Lani, while simultaneously being intrigued by this new woman, Gregor parked his Cruiser and headed into the bar.

Time to meet the vixen.

Chapter Three

෩

Lani stood just outside the Green Island Bar and paused to collect her thoughts. She carried her satchel slung casually over her shoulder and packed with a girl's necessities—a beamer, some travel food and bottles of vitawater, and a couple changes of clothes. She had no idea how hard or easy it would be to track down and retrieve Leif, but she always believed in being prepared.

She also had a sheaf of papers inside a marked folder covering all the information she could find about the Xylone Amazons and their practices. As another intoxicated man stumbled from the bar, she couldn't help the wry grin cross her face.

If even half the information she had collected turned out to be true, *poor* Leif would be having the time of his life. Eighteen and just blossoming into his sexuality, she had serious doubts that even if she turned up to *rescue* him the man would willingly come back with her.

Amazon tribes had been around literally for hundreds of thousands of years, apparently coming from one of the sections of old Earth. Centuries ago, after Earth's men and women had begun to travel the galaxy, the planet formerly known as Earth had been pretty much imploded by two major opposing countries.

The galaxy had learned a number of important lessons, the two main ones being no planet was indestructible, and differing political and religious beliefs were a major cause of friction between inhabitants.

While much of the other planets throughout the galaxy had very far-back ancestry rooted from original Earth inhabitants, it wasn't something most people cared to admit to or discuss. The Amazonian women were fiercely proud of their heritage, and pretty much put all of their "nonconforming" traditions down to being "from Earth".

Considering not a single *captive* to date had wanted to press charges of any kind — other than the occasional youthful swain desperate to marry or bond with some poor Amazon woman who was refusing — most planets throughout the galaxy gave the Amazons their free rein.

Consisting of women, the tribes had learned to take their men where they could, and use them to impregnate the younger members. Male children were either returned to the fathers, or raised in the Amazon-led orphanages. Female children were raised to become future Amazons.

There appeared, particularly in the last five years, reports on how the masculine children moved up in the business world, obviously not affected in the slightest from being raised in the specialist orphanages, and how a small number of Amazon women did leave the tribe to further careers elsewhere. Yet for the most part the women were perfectly happy to continue as they had for many thousands of years.

Of course there were a few more obscure documents on the deviant and dominating sexual practices of the Amazons. But even these references were made in glowing terms, very satisfied men boasting of how many women in one night they were able to perform for and how being the sexual *slave* of an Amazon woman turned out to be even better than their horniest dreams.

While Lani had no idea if Leif had ever indulged in a submissive fantasy in his life, she was extremely confident the Amazons wouldn't want to hurt or injure him, and most likely would pamper him inside as well as outside the bedroom. Even if she hadn't been going to ask Gregor for his help in rescuing her godson, she would now need to ask his help, as she thought it likely she would need to bodily carry the young man from the tribe.

Shaking her head, realizing she had been standing outside daydreaming for nearly five minutes, Lani took a deep breath and entered the bar.

Dim lights hid what she would place a large number of credits on proving to be a step-up-from-a-dive old style tavern. Crowded tables and chairs bumped against each other in the small main room. A number of games of chance were set up in one corner, the telltale wisps of smoke curling from a few sources.

Barely clad femservers carried trays and wiggled their assets. While it wasn't obvious there were rooms to rent in the back, Lani would be astounded if it proved less than two of the servers she saw serving assorted drinks and nibbles wouldn't doubled out the back as escorts.

After looking closely at four or five of them, Lani relaxed. At least none of these femservers looked to be under eighteen. She hated seeing how young some kids now chose to become rich faster by taking a sideline nowadays.

Moving in from the door, Lani hugged the wall, wanting to scout the area and find Gregor before she moved over to him. Smiling to herself, she admitted she also wanted to catch her breath and think about what she would say.

Before she could fully scout out the room, a large body brushed against hers. Automatically letting her hand fall down to her beamer, Lani clasped it and moved to feint defensively to the side before she could even halt the action. *Too much training,* she wryly admitted to herself.

"Take it easy, Lani," a familiar, deeply husky voice crooned to her, making her want to melt. "It's just me."

Lani took a deep breath and tried to calm her racing heart. She turned to face the man she had come to meet and looked up at him.

"Sorry, Gregor, I didn't see you and I don't like people creeping up on me. You're lucky we're not in some back alley. You'd have been stunned or worse by now."

Lani couldn't help the heat that pooled in her skinsuit pants at the sexy, devilish grin that lightened Gregor's features. The silver eyes flashed and she knew he felt humor about her words.

"I'll count myself lucky then. What are you doing here?"

His words seemed so casual, yet she could feel the pressure of his eyes, feel the intensity of his stare all the way through her body. She shrugged, hoping she seemed casual and not like a fumbling schoolgirl asking her first date to the star-prom. Without thinking, she moved a hand to push a stray curl behind her ear, only to find her hair properly bound back into its ponytail.

Hating the telling gesture, Lani cleared her throat.

"I sent the vixen to you, so I'm just honoring the meeting I offered. I created that code and needed to test it out on someone who would understand just how potentially useful it would be. Can we go somewhere to talk? Do you have a table here?"

Lani could feel her face heat slightly, and knew she was inexplicably grateful for the dim light of the tavern. She only hoped Gregor couldn't smell her desire or taste the sexual hunger that emanated from her and hung in the air between them.

He looked her up and down for a short moment. Lani felt her nipples peak and rasp gently against her skinsuit. A lock of his blond hair fell over his eyes, creating the strangest desire in her to tenderly brush it back for him. Licking her dry lips, Lani desperately tried to ignore his sleek muscles as they bulged beneath his skinsuit.

Try as she might to ignore the sexual attraction between them, Lani couldn't help it as she tried to force moisture into her dry mouth. She couldn't remember the last time she had such strong physical reactions to the force of her sexual hunger. Maybe in her teens?

As his silver eyes finally lifted to clash with her own green ones, she could see the deep flare of the sexual hunger still residing there. She could feel herself dampen even more at the realization he definitely wanted her too, no matter how hard he tried to ignore her.

Smiling, letting out a breath of relief, Lani knew a small measure of control had just been slipped back to her. She might be melting into a puddle of sexual need and frustration right here in front of the goddess and everyone present, but Gregor wanted her just as badly as well—and that boded well for her.

"Yeah," he drawled, it took Lani a moment to remember what she had asked. "I have a table here. Let's go sit and talk."

Smiling slightly, she turned to follow Gregor as he led them through the throng of people to a small table near the back of the tavern.

Lani sat down opposite him, her blush deepening as their legs brushed past each other under the small table. Clearing her throat, determined to at least try to stay in control tonight, she picked up the bottle of vitawater already sitting on the table and poured herself and Gregor a glass.

"I hope you don't feel like I've used you," she began, sipping her drink to keep her throat wet and give her hands something to do. "I just wanted to have the very best person try to crack my code. You're most certainly the best I know."

Lani shrugged, looked back up into those piecing gray eyes. Gregor simply sat there, patient as a saint. He obviously waited for her to explain everything to him. His predatory, waiting stare only slightly unnerved her. Instead of making her feel gauche or uncomfortable, it actually just seemed to turn her on more.

Would he be this patient in bed? Draw her out? Pit her own desires and needs against her so she ended up turning herself on more with her own desire?

In a heartbeat, Lani decided she didn't want to be the same as every other woman he seduced like this. She had heaps of confidence in herself. Either he'd take her as she was, or not at all. She decided in a split second to challenge him instead of playing by his rules.

"Do you always use this trick on women? Simply wait for them to work themselves into a fever pitch and confess all their sins or needs before you? Gotta tell you, it's one helluva strategy."

Gregor smiled, his features even more beautiful with the flash of white teeth.

"Is it working?" He seemed truly interested in her response.

"A little," she admitted, lowering her eyes and shifting to try and ease the ache between her legs, but only reminding her of how damp it had become down there, "but I've been through worse."

She looked up at him, let her eyes clash with his to show she wasn't some cowardly maiden. She looked him straight in the eyes as she laid down her plans.

"I think I've created a fantastic code and I want Management to at least look at it, if not use it. But we both know to even be looked at, let alone considered by Management, it will need your stamp of approval."

Lani took a deep breath. She didn't know if she wanted to admit she wanted to get his attention. Yet she knew if she didn't say so now, she would seem cowardly, as the electricity sparking between them was enough to light an entire planet.

"I also wanted to get your attention, which I think you've worked out by now. But something else has come up since then."

Lani took a deep breath and didn't let her eyes waver from his. He seemed partly amused, partly intrigued, partly...*interested*? She couldn't really tell, and so she tried to get her heart to stop beating so fast. Gregor's gaze lay heavy and hot over her. It created a strange sort of intimacy, as if this were a bizarre form of foreplay between them.

Lani smiled at the odd thought, in a strange sense letting it calm her. His gaze felt so heavy she likened it to his body braced over her during the intimacies of sex.

She could feel his touch on her skin as if his soul or spirit reached out and trailed hot hands over her breasts and down her belly. Her nipples peaked again and she prayed he couldn't see or wouldn't be able to tell.

"Go on, Lani," he said. His voice was a raspy, husky tone that, more than anything, proved his interest and desire for her. His eyes hadn't strayed from hers, but she instinctively knew he had looked his fill of her heavy breasts, the nipples erect and rasping tightly over the skin of her suit.

For one insane moment Lani imagined stripping the suit from her body and climbing up onto the table that separated them. A little cheer group started up in the back of her head.

"*Fuck him, fuck him, fuck him,*" they chanted, over and over. As she imagined herself climbing up onto the table and spreading her bare legs wide, imagined herself touching her erect clit and rubbing the need away, Lani bit her lip to stop her own moan and squeezed her legs together. She needed to come badly now, and her imagination was not helping her ease her need in the slightest.

The cheer group in her mind didn't even pause for breath.

"*Take me now! Take me now! Take me now!*" they chanted, imagining a naked Gregor rise up and grab her hips, thrusting balls-deep inside her. Lani swallowed the moan that rose with the wicked images playing through her mind.

Realizing she was one heated thrust away from climax, and the man had only looked at her and set her imagination soaring, she became aware of the fact that she must look like a complete moron. What the hell had she been saying to him?

When Gregor leaned forward, his gaze held steadily on hers, she jerked slightly as his hand took her chin between his fingers. He leaned so close to her, she could taste his breath as he breathed gently over her.

"Darling," he drawled softly, so only her ears could hear him, "we can't possibly fuck wildly here on the table. A few regulations about public displays of affection, lewd contact, and I bet for good measure we'd be slapped with disturbing the peace."

Lani's strange sense of humor surfaced to the top, bubbling away as always. "But we'd give them one hell of an eyeful."

She couldn't believe it as Gregor chuckled. Mostly people didn't understand her sense of humor. It was dark and often a very dry, sarcastic sense of wit. The fact he understood and even appreciated it by the dark glint in his eyes and husky chuckles only added fuel to her fire.

If she wasn't careful she knew she could fall ass over heels in love with this man. And that would be a disaster. She had tried love once, and the entire experience had been nothing but ridiculous and painful. She didn't want a repeat performance. Better to keep this as sex.

"Much as I would love to spread you out on this table, and even do whatever other fantasies are playing behind those expressive eyes of yours, my dear," he continued, as his eyes bored into hers, "and I *do* want to try a few of those fantasies out, you mentioned something else 'coming up' between you sending that delicious vixen and now."

Recalled to her request, Lani blinked the lust from her eyes. She smiled sassily, back in control of herself again.

"It's the cheer group in the back of my head. They're pumping my body up, screaming for...well, never mind that. My godson seems to have been taken by a group of Amazons on Xylone. I've done a ton of research on them—" Lani missed whatever expression crossed Gregor's eyes at her words, as she was shuffling inside her bag looking for the folder of research she had compiled.

Gregor interrupted her words and dual trains of thought—the cheerleaders were back with even more naughty suggestions of seducing him by completing herself first. The images of her own fingers stroking her clit and screaming in ecstasy while Gregor looked on at her hungrily were distracting to say the least.

Finally his words penetrated her brain and her mind organized itself. The cheerleaders were once again pushed to the back.

"Xylone? *You're* the godmother Leif Bardobos contacted?"

Lani blinked again, her mind whirling to keep up with Gregor and his mind. "Yeah. You know about this?"

Gregor shrugged and Lani smiled. She had found her opening. Research she excelled in. Crossing her legs under the table, wincing slightly as her leg brushed his, she kept her mind focused. Even though they were both fully clothed, she would have to have been dead and buried to *not* feel the electricity sparkle between them. They might as well be naked for all the use their clothes did to protect each other from their crackle.

"Talk to me, Gregor," she insisted.

Gregor shrugged lazily, a huge mountain lion of old, indulging himself in a whim.

"My best friend and I…investigate, I suppose you could say, certain cases which don't seem to resolve properly." Lani nodded, knowing well the feeling of frustration and annoyance when a superior told you to drop something. A lot of brick walls and black marks began to occur if one didn't drop said subject. For her short time on the Force she had a few black marks of her own. Lani never had been able to leave well enough alone.

"Max received some of Leif's information. He seems fine, and I seriously doubt he's doing anything except fucking himself raw."

Lani sensed an utterly alien shaft of pure jealousy flash through her. Taken completely by surprise, she shifted on her seat. She listened as Gregor continued.

"The Amazons won't hurt him. If anything he'll be having the time of his life. Frankly I'm jealous of the kid."

Lani smiled. "I take it you're going after him?" When Gregor nodded, she rested her arms on the table, unconsciously leaning farther forward and displaying her breasts, to look him directly in the eye.

"I want to come along with you. This was the other thing I needed. I can help, and if necessary I can convince Leif to come back with us. If he's having such a ball, he won't want to come back. Let me come with you."

At the sudden flare of heat in Gregor's eyes, she felt a blush creep up her face again at the realization of her words. Damned milk-white Irish skin! Her great-grandmother might have been pure Old Irish, but she didn't see any dilution of the pale features or red-hot blushes all those generations had given.

"Okay, so I also want to fuck you until I can't walk. We can work around that. But first we need to strike a deal. I'm packed. I have my bag here under the table. Surely you'll need help? Here I am volunteering."

Lani held her breath, looked deeply into the molten silver of Gregor's eyes. She had an incredibly strong urge to offer up promises, to splay herself before him. Yet she did neither. She didn't want to dig her hole deeper, or offer too much if he were just toying with her. For all she knew he had meant to ask her along anyway.

After a moment of tense, sex-crackling tension and silence, Gregor leaned forward onto the table as well. Eye to eye, barely a hairsbreadth separating them, his words ran hot and molten, just like the river of desire between them.

"You follow my orders," he started, his eyes hot, roaming over her features. "When I say move, you move. When I say get down, you eat the dust." Lani couldn't help herself, she had to tease him. She raised her eyebrow.

"I don't follow orders very well, G." At the intimate nickname, she saw surprise and even more heat fill his eyes. His pupils dilated slightly, and Lani knew no matter what else occurred, she had found a feminine weapon. She could feel even more heat pool between her legs as Gregor reached out to hold her chin again.

"Oh, Lani," he panted, a slight sexual flush creeping up his neck, "you will *love* following orders. I do believe that was a whopper of a lie there, little girl." Lani couldn't help the tiny whimper of need that escaped her lips.

The endearment made her pussy leak even more cream. No one had ever called her a *little girl*—and at nearly six-foot tall she had felt far from little since she turned ten years old. But the manner Gregor caressed the term, the lilting cadence of his tone as he purred it made her want to strip there and then.

The cheering squad came back with a vengeance.

"I do believe you'll love to follow my lead, my orders. In return, I'll give you the best fucking of your lifetime. I'll do anything and everything you've ever fantasized about. We'll burn the sheets up, and you'll be walking like a penguin before we even reach Xylone. Do you know what that will feel like, *little girl*?"

Her eyes glazed, her mind filled with erotic scenes no man would ever dare do to her. She saw him suckling her clit, his dark blond head resting between her splayed thighs. She saw herself watch his face as he gently inserted one lubed finger into her ass. She saw herself laid out over his lap, being spanked, and then having her ass reamed.

Scenario after scenario of each and every one of her dark fantasies flashed before her eyes, all in the space of a minute. Lani couldn't help but moan and close her eyes as Gregor moved that last inch forward and kissed her fiercely, obviously knowing some of what was being portrayed behind her eyes.

His lips pressed down firmly and warmly over hers. He pressed with strength but still managed to be so soft she moaned in desire and approval. He didn't open himself to her, didn't dive forward. This obviously was only his preliminary scouting mission, yet his sense of impatience and urgency made his kiss firm, demanding, utterly decadent and sexy.

Lips soft, he pressed against her, breathing in her scent. Lani reached her hand around to cup his head, to draw him closer and urge him deeper inside her. Even across the small table, she wished they could press chest to chest. Her hands cupped his head, one hand easily running through the silky strands of his blond hair, thin, soft and perfect.

Just as she could feel the furnace inside her begin to ignite, Gregor opened his mouth and she enjoyed the thrust of his tongue, hot and wet, slip inside her. He tasted salty, masculine and very faintly of Blue Vodka. He must have had a shot while waiting for her to arrive. She had been surprised by how long it had taken her to walk to the small tavern, resulting in her being a few minutes late.

Before she could truly begin to taste him, to explore him, he pulled away.

Lani moaned, this time in disappointment, then bit her lips softly shut. She opened her eyes, unaware of when she had even closed them.

Gregor watched her, his dark, hooded expression revealing more than he could know. He had nearly lost control, and Lani would place a ton of credits on the fact he wouldn't have liked that small loss.

"Oh yeah, little girl. You're going to love following my orders."

Lani shivered, both from the naughty sensation his nickname sent through her, as well as the knowledge she would indeed love following his sexual orders. In the field, however, she would follow her own instincts and thoughts.

No man ruled her.

She smiled, not wanting to start *that* particular argument any time soon.

"Shall we head back to your place to pack, G?" she asked. Her voice sounded low, sexy, husky from the desire and the dryness of her throat. She licked her lips, amazed she could still taste him, and she loved it.

"Sure thing, but remember, I'm in charge here."

Lani couldn't help the sarcastic smile any more than she could help breathing. Teasing this large, imposing man was far too easy and too right to not do.

"Of course," she said mockingly, knowing in her heart even though she had little experience of this sort in the field, she would still follow her own instincts. What woman in her right mind wouldn't? Besides, they were dealing with a bunch of Amazons, a bunch of *women*. Who better to deal with them than another woman?

"I commed in my request for leave on the way here. Have you secured the okay from on high to do this?"

Gregor pierced her with a look. She smiled sweetly in return. She had merely been *asking*, which was no sin the last time she checked.

The man merely grunted and rose to leave. Lani smiled to herself and picked up her own small bag to follow him outside the tavern. Lani noticed a number of men and women glance idly her way as they left.

The women would linger on Gregor's impressive physique, and then look her up and down, obviously wondering how *she* could be leaving with him. She felt her face broaden its grin as she realized she obviously held status in leaving with such a handsome specimen of male anatomy.

Gregor, meanwhile, seemed utterly oblivious to all the stares, male and female, as they left the small tavern. Out on the street, however, he walked next to her in step as he led her a few paces down the seedy street. He beeped open a Cruiser and held the door open for her as she climbed in.

Belting herself in, she smiled secretively. She had no idea what the future held, but by Gregor's side, she had a certainty that it would be pretty damn interesting and exciting. The rumbling purr of the engine moved through the practically brand-new Cruiser. Lani shifted her legs, wishing her erect clit would cease throbbing and her soaked panties wouldn't remind her of just how much she desired this man that coupled with the rumbling purr of the machine they sat within was sending her system close to overload.

Lani shot a brief look over at Gregor as he drove. Much like how he did everything else, he drove in a calm, cool and controlled manner. Gregor easily maneuvered the Cruiser wherever he wished it to go.

Lani smiled. Unlike the Cruiser, she had a mind and will of her own. It would certainly be interesting being maneuvered by Gregor, but she doubted she would always submit as beautifully or as easily as the top-of-the-line machine currently under his hands.

She smiled. The trip ahead would undoubtedly prove to be full of pleasure and excitement.

Chapter Four

∞

Gregor pulled his Cruiser into the driveway of his lodgings. As he parked it, he concentrated on small details so he wouldn't turn and pull Lani into his embrace.

"Do you own it?" she queried as she pulled off her safety belt.

Gregor smiled into the darkness.

"As much as anyone ever does," he stated and gratefully removed his own safety belt and climbed out. "Come on," he urged, "we have a really early start tomorrow, or rather, today."

As Lani walked up next to him on the path Gregor restarted the safety device on the Cruiser which he had personally created.

Weary from his long day, Gregor led them both up to his lodging. He was grateful yet again for the darkness. His gardens were bare. Perfectly manicured grass, but no flowers or shrubs or other assorted *pretty* things adorned his walkway. He didn't really know if Lani appreciated pretty gardens, but he still knew a great relief that she wouldn't be able to see just how bare his yard was.

Strange, but he had never worried about that sort of thing before. Kyli had merely teased him the few times she and Max had visited him here, and no other woman ever seemed to register enough for him to be able to remember their reactions.

Gregor frowned.

He knew he had an exceedingly strong attraction to Lani, but that didn't really explain his interest in posing or showing off his toys to her. Quickly, he deactivated his house alarm and led her in to the main living area.

Tapping the side of the doorframe to activate the lights as he entered the main room, he looked around in a quick sweep. There were a few scattered items here and there, but nothing to be too embarrassed over.

"I'll be just a few minutes. I'll pack my bag and check the sheets on the spare bed." Gregor caught Lani's eye. If the hot look within the emerald green depths was anything to go by, she felt exactly the same level of desire as he. Striding over to her, he tilted her chin with one hand and lowered his head.

Kissing her hungrily, fiercely, he relished the press of his lips against hers. He darted his tongue out, swiping a taste of her spicy femininity. Without meaning to, he inhaled deeply. She smelled of hunger and heat. The scent of old-world flowers tingled as he brought it deep down inside himself. Jasmine maybe?

Before he could lose himself in her intoxicating taste and feminine smell, he pulled away. He had a moment where he felt a flush of masculine pride and satisfaction well deep within him. Lani blinked, as if awakening from a dream, or to try and brush dizziness of his touch aside. He was stoked to realize he affected her just as much as she did him.

"I'll be just a sec," he said huskily, clearing his throat. "Make yourself at home. The spare bedroom is second door on your left down the hall but just let me check it out first. I should only be a couple of minutes." With that Gregor stepped out of the room to pack and clear his head.

Barely able to breathe, so deeply did he feel desire for Lani, Gregor mentally made his list. He stormed down the hallway and into the master bedroom. Gregor pushed the thought of "Master" from his mind and concentrated fiercely on the task at hand.

He pulled his working pack and the spare box of supplies from the bottom of his closet. Checking the first aid and survival kits, he mentally ran through the work checklist as he opened the box of spare supplies. He kept a number of items in reserve for times like this when he had to leave on practically no notice.

Five minutes later after packing from his drawers and cabinets, he came back to the box and added new food kits and supplies, a couple of changes of clothes and other essential items he always packed when going on the hunt.

Desperately wanting to cleanse the smell of smoke and alcohol from his body from the tavern, but knowing he needed to take care of Lani first, he dropped his bag on the floor by the door and crossed over the hall to the spare room.

In quick succession he checked to see that the sheets were clean and the spare blankets were within easy reach.

Satisfied, he retraced his steps back to the main living area. He found Lani in front of one wall, staring at a painted series of three erotic scenes he had, in his lust-riddled thoughts, forgotten graced his wall. Lani seemed interested and curious about the scenes, not offended or outraged. Not wanting to delve into explanations, Gregor cleared his throat.

"Your room is ready. There's a small cleansing chamber leading just off the side. You should find everything there. If you're hungry the kitchen is just through there," he indicated a door on the other side of the room. "Feel free to help yourself. Otherwise I'll wake you up in a couple of hours when it's time for us to head to the Port."

Lani turned silently away from the paintings on his wall to face him, and for the first time that evening, Gregor acknowledged the clawing hunger he could so obviously read in Lani's eyes. A shaft of lust unlike anything he had ever experienced slashed straight through him. He now understood this edgy, restless feeling that had plagued him all evening. He wanted Lani more than anything he had ever previously known, and considering his many, *many* years of sexual exploring, that was quite a feat.

Making a snap decision, he closed the few paces between them. Surprisingly, Lani closed the final step before he could. When she grabbed his waist, aligning his iron-hard cock with her heat he couldn't help the moan of fierce need that escaped his lips.

"Your pictures," she gasped, breathless with lust.

"Later," he moaned. All he wanted to do was kiss her again, drink in the smell of nearly forgotten jasmine and taste her spicy need. He plunged himself into her, wishing he could merge their bodies, climb right into her and wallow there for a decade or so.

As she arched up into him, one hand snaked around her back and dragged her closer, crushed her against his chest and the length of his body. His other hand angled her head so he could press his lips and tongue as deeply into her as possible.

Gregor moaned and led Lani a step toward the hall. Even as he sated himself, he could feel the clawing hunger deeply embedded in his chest, not to mention the fierce pressure in his fully aroused cock roaring for release.

He wanted everything from this woman. Wanted her trust and her need. He wanted to entice her into his deepest, darkest thoughts and fantasies. He wanted to initiate her fully into his own private world and give her everything he had to give. No woman had ever been able to take his all.

He knew he was a dark, hungry man. Not only did he want absolutely everything from his partner, but he always stood willing to give his all in return. Most women couldn't give their all, let alone deal with everything of his.

Lani, he knew deep within his bones, would be different. She would *demand* everything he had, and give herself and all she was in return. They were alike in that manner. They would either set the world on fire with their passion and joint need, or tear each other to pieces.

It would prove most interesting.

Reluctantly, in small movements, Gregor pulled himself away.

"We *will* sleep in different rooms tonight, or we won't be refreshed enough to start the mission. It's a long flight to Xylone. We'll need all our energy."

For a moment, he thought Lani would argue with him. Then a femininely calculating look came into her eye and she nodded without saying a word.

Contrarily, he suddenly wanted Lani's skin against him, wanted to feel her come against his cock, his mouth, his fingers. Smiling ruthlessly, he gently grabbed her hand and pulled her out into the hallway.

She snickered, but didn't utter a word for which he was inexplicably grateful. Gregor pulled her through his room and into his cleansing chamber. Stripping off his shoes in seconds, he turned on and adjusted the chamber to an acceptable temperature.

Turning back to Lani, eyes wide with surprise and desire, he smiled wickedly.

"We *will* sleep separately, since we both need the rest. But there's no sense in wasting the water."

In one quick movement, he removed his skinsuit, smiling wickedly in a taunting, utterly masculine challenge. He could feel his already hard cock stiffen even more as Lani slowly nodded and removed her own skinsuit much more seductively and with far greater skill than he had bothered with.

Watching her toe off her shoes seemed strangely erotic, something he had never realized before. Even with her slow, seductive movements, purposely geared to tease and entice him, within seconds she stood before him, naked and perfect.

When she cocked her head to one side, he snapped out of the semi-trance he had been in. Opening the door to the cleansing chamber, he gallantly waved an arm.

"After you, my dear," he insisted in the age-old courtly way. As Lani's soft, hot flesh brushed past his, he clamped down on a groan.

He knew this would be a journey he would never forget.

Quickly, so as not to let any more heat escape, he followed her into the small chamber and closed the door behind them with a small *click*.

He smiled broadly as the heat and steam enveloped him. No matter what the future might bring, he knew he would always remember this small pocket of time he had carved out to fulfill as many fantasies as he possibly could.

Chapter Five

ဆ

Lani closed her eyes for a moment and enjoyed the sensation of having the water and steam pound on her skin. She had purposely chosen to have separate water and steam chambers, yet she also enjoyed having both together like Gregor obviously had.

She realized closing her eyes only heightened her awareness of the heat and strength of Gregor's chest and torso behind her. She inhaled deeply, slowly, trying to calm her mind and body. Yet the air seemed filled with the steam from the chamber, with the woodsy, purely masculine scent of Gregor.

Opening her eyes slowly, torn between wanting to keep them closed and burning all the sensations and feelings into her memory, but also not wanting to miss a single moment visually, Lani enjoyed the strange sensation of their combined chemistry and sexual attraction prickling over her skin.

A part of her knew the mingled chemistry and desperate sexual attraction between them was pure lust. Yet she also wondered if some of the electricity between them was the heightened survival instinct she couldn't help but feel just like an animal would sense when its mate drew near. She had read many years ago that a human's body, once upon a time, had been geared toward physically recognizing its mate, its life partner. Maybe she was a throwback to a bygone era?

Or maybe, her mind injected cynically, *you just have an overactive imagination like some stupid Ancient romance heroine and will soon shriek and faint from the dastardly deeds the evil hero wants to perform on you.*

Lani smiled to herself. She had often wanted the evil bad guy, to turn him into some noble hero and have him ravish her. It had been a common failing of her back in her teens, to fall for the pirate, spacecowboy or other villain.

Shaking her head, trying hard not to laugh at her silly thoughts, she dunked her head under the spray, hoping to wash away her ridiculous thoughts along with the water.

Her body quivered as Gregor's strong, muscled arms passed by her to grab the container of cleansing lotion. Tiny frissons of electric current zinged through her body at the sensitive contact. The heat and desire pooled in her pussy, making her wet and want to squirm.

She half turned to watch the slight play of muscles along his arms and chest as he squirted a handful of the lotion onto his palm. She took the bottle from him and tried not to feel incredible envy as his hand roamed over his chest, angling down toward his massively erect cock. She squirted her own dollop of the cleanser onto her palm, replaced it in its holder, and began to sensually rub the lotion into her neck and shoulders.

"Here," Gregor's husky voice came from behind her. She shivered at the wet, fluid contact of his skin on hers. "Let me help you."

Lani opened her mouth, to tell him she could easily clean her own body. But the sweet sensation of his hand on her skin, the slight roughness of his palm catching on her softer skin had her quickly drawing in a breath and trying not to melt into a puddle on the floor.

Gregor's hands cupped her aching breasts, the pad of one of his thumbs running over her nipple, making it stand out even more proudly and erect than before. Lani couldn't help herself. She moaned and turned in toward the fiery heat of Gregor's body.

She shivered at the sensations he sent coursing through her body, and let her hands run down his torso, memorizing the sculpted mass of muscles. She enjoyed the journey her hands made down the flat smoothness of his belly until her hands reached and automatically circled the thick length of his straining erection.

Her body seemed to move on instinct, as if she had known this man forever and done this many, many times before. She didn't realize her eyes had closed, it seemed like some instinct took over her. Her thoughts were a wild jumble of images, yet Gregor's face, the deep-seated hunger in those burning gray eyes seemed to almost haunt her.

Her eyes snapped open again. She didn't care that they were supposed to be working together, even if it was in an unofficial capacity. She didn't care she could likely be reassigned to another division if Management heard about her activities. She wanted Gregor more than anything else, and right in that moment, she didn't care about any potential fallout from her actions.

Stepping mentally back within the small chamber, Lani slowly closed her hands over Gregor's much larger ones. Raising an eyebrow, she gently opened his hands and removed them from her aching nipples.

"Lani—" he started. She hushed him, wanted to do this *her* way. She eased his hands down to his sides, letting them hang there. Then she bent down and kneeled before him on the steam-slickened floor of the chamber.

Lani didn't need his indrawn breath to know he understood what she had in mind. He would have to be incredibly stupid not to know. Her head and mouth sat level with his straining cock, mere inches away from his thick, eagerly quivering erection.

Lani licked her lips and heard a strangled, muted groan come from Gregor.

About to lean forward and take his entire head into her mouth, she smiled as an eager hand clasped the back of her head, delving his fingers through her damp hair.

"I fantasized about this," Gregor hoarsely confided. "I fantasized you were sucking me as I jerked myself off. You gonna make my fantasy come true, little girl?"

Lani smiled. "Seems like it. I think the idea has merit, don't you, G?"

Lani couldn't help but smirk as Gregor could only moan his approval and draw her nearer his staff. Lani opened her lips and relished the hot, silky feel of his cock as it entered her mouth. She closed her eyes for a moment, wanting to savor the sensation of his first penetration of her body.

The salty taste she had been expecting wasn't there. She realized it had been washed away by the water. He tasted clean and the thin skin covering his erection seemed impossibly hot. She enjoyed the feel of him in her mouth, thick and masculine.

Lani relaxed her throat and sucked him as far down into herself as she could. Swiping her tongue around his length, she very, very carefully grazed her teeth along the stalk of his shaft. He moaned and a thrill of excitement sang through her as his hand tightened its hold on her head. Gregor pulled her farther down onto himself.

She stroked him up and down, sucked him down her throat as she changed the pressure within her mouth. Lani wanted to give him as much pleasure as possible, so she used all her skill.

Lani raised her eyes, wanting to watch Gregor as she sucked him. His face seemed drawn, his eyes hot and devouring. His gaze rested on her intensely.

"Keep going, little girl, suck me dry. *Please*," he moaned as she drew particularly hard down on his shaft, creating a blend of pleasure and needful pain.

Lani had never felt this level of womanly power, she grinned her delight at the interesting sensation of having this much control over the infamous Gregor. Women from other departments whispered about his prowess, how he easily topped any other man as a lover. How he never gave up control and had an almost psychic knowledge of what would pleasure a woman most and best.

Having him in her mouth, having control of the lovemaking, was a heady thing, exciting and exhilarating at the same time. Lani never wanted it to end.

But she could feel the heat and anticipation gather in his balls, could feel them rise slightly of their own accord. She knew he would blow soon, and so she gently tickled the tight sac, hoping to stretch the moment out just a bit. Instead, her teasing actions elicited yet another moan from Gregor.

Stroking the underside of his balls, sucking deeply on his shaft she smiled around the massive stem as he groaned incoherently.

"Lani... I'm going to... I can't..."

Not even bothering to reply, Lani continued to suck and stroke, not letting up on her rhythm. *No Mercy* was one of the Force's rules. She tried not to laugh at just how relevant it seemed here and now.

Mere seconds later Gregor shouted hoarsely. He fisted both his hands on her head and pressed her down onto his cock even farther. Breathing steadily Lani accepted even more of his cock down her throat, swallowing convulsively as he shot his seed deep into her stomach.

She would have groaned in unison with him if she could have managed it around his shaft. As it was, only smothered moans could escape her mouth, humming enticingly against the sensitive skin, making him shout out and spurt even more of his cum down her throat.

Now he tasted salty and masculine, just as she had known he would. He still tasted clean and wet, but he also had that musky, masculine saltiness to him she had been expecting all along.

She licked around the head of his cock, enjoying the last few seconds of control she had with him. Before she wanted to, she was being lifted by strong hands under the shoulders and plastered against the warmly tiled wall of the chamber.

Wet, heated masculinity pressed against every inch of her flesh.

"That was fantastic," he purred, sated and replete. "I most definitely owe you for that one."

Lani merely smiled and licked the last of his taste from her lips. She certainly wouldn't be complaining. She'd had a barrel of laughs herself.

"But now," he continued darkly, "I do believe it's time for me to return the favor and cleanse you."

Very gently he bent his head down slightly, teasing her as if he would kiss her but still holding his head back. He pressed her hips back into the warmth of the cubicle walls with his own slim hips. Lani looked up into his face as his chest pressed against her naked breasts. Her breath caught as she looked deeply into his eyes.

In the gray depths shone myriad emotions...heat, desire, a deeply seated lust and a twinkling wickedness, a knowing she ached to discover. She wanted to learn all about herself, wanted to delve into her secrets and desires with this man.

It had been years since she had last had a lover she wanted so desperately, whom she had the luxury of moving slowly with. In this modern day and age, particularly with all the restrictions on a member of the Force, most couplings were quick, heated and only marginally satisfying. Over before they could begin.

It had been an age since Lani had been able to take her time, discover more about herself as well as her lover. Anything other than which places on his, or her, body were sensitive took too much time and effort. The last few years in particular she had been working and studying so hard to make it onto the Force, she had barely had time to take care of herself, let alone keep a half-serious relationship flourishing.

Now seemed to be the perfect time to seduce and be seduced by Gregor, to discover more about herself and her sexual desires. She also looked forward to learning not only every inch of skin on Gregor's body, but also what he could do for her as a lover, what knowledge about herself and a man she could take with her when their time came to an end.

Her willingness must have shown in her eyes, or by some nonphysical means, for Gregor bent his head down so his lips pressed against her eager ones. She felt his hair-roughened thigh gently pry her legs apart, until she stood splayed against the wall. Eagerly, she opened herself up to him, opened her body to anything they could do together in their allotted time.

"Do you really want this, Lani?" Gregor said huskily in her ear. "'Cause once I start, it might take a while for both of us to sate ourselves."

Lani moaned. With Gregor pressing her against the warmth of the wall, with the woodsy scent of him on her skin and in her nose, she could barely even remember her last lover, let alone one who had taken his time to seduce and prepare her even half as well as Gregor was doing.

By and large her couplings had been rushed and frenzied. The sex had been over-eager and almost forced, as if they were both on a timer. Half the time *her* completion had been far down the agenda, and even once she'd had to take matters into her own hands, literally, after the man had left.

Suffice to say she had never seen *him* again, and she certainly had no doubts that nothing resembling that farce would be happening here, tonight, with Gregor!

"I want to start this, Gregor," she said to him, absolute certainty ringing in her voice. "The real question is, are you prepared to finish it? Completion for a woman, as I have discovered, is rather different than completion for a man."

Lani loved his dry, deep chuckle. It seemed as if it were torn from the deepest part of his soul, as if it sprung from so far inside him it was dark and light simultaneously. An interesting conundrum—just like the man it came from.

"Ah, little Lani. How you do tempt me. Let me show you how deep my understanding is for the satisfaction of a woman."

Before Lani could question him further, he had rested his hands on her hips and kneeled down onto the floor of the chamber. Somehow he managed to spread her legs farther apart while simultaneously pressing her even more deeply against the wall, splaying her before him like some ancient, pagan, sacrificial feast.

Even though the chamber temperature was perfectly warm, Lani could feel goose bumps begin to cover her arms. She felt wanton, wicked, as if she were truly some goddess incarnate about to be ravished by the Dark God of her choosing.

She couldn't help but look down at Gregor's dark blond head, damp from the heat and water spray. When he lifted his face to meet hers, she felt her breath catch in her throat.

His eyes were the darkest metal gray she had ever seen, like a storm-cloud before it burst, or just before lightning erupted from it. She searched so intensely into his eyes it took a moment for her to register how close his mouth sat to her creaming pussy. When his tongue flashed out of his mouth, she likened him to a cat lapping cream.

The rough sensitivity of his tongue registered along all the nerve endings surrounding her clit, and her back arched involuntarily. She gasped, unable to form a coherent word.

Again and again Gregor lapped and buried his face in the secret warmth of her pussy, lapping and stroking. His tongue acted as if it were a sentient being, knowing exactly when to caress her engorged clit, and when to dodge it and tease her.

His smooth, thick fingers teased her outer labia, stroking her into a frenzy of passion and need. So desperate did she feel to need something extra inside her she couldn't even hear her own pleas as her ears seemed to be buzzing with the rush of blood and need inside her body.

She nearly screamed, thankfully choking it off at the last second, when he finally plunged two fingers knuckle-deep inside her. The fullness, the stretching, decadent feeling nearly had her coming well before her time.

Lani canted her hips in time to the sensual rhythm Gregor set. She thrust her hips as far forward as she could manage for every push his fingers and tongue took. Lani wanted to watch him desperately, to watch the sweat gleam on his gorgeous face as he licked and sucked her clit. She wanted to watch the changing color in his eyes and to see the deep-seated need inside him. Yet all too soon the needs inside her body overcame everything else around her and she had to close her eyes to try and gain more control.

To think, she said to herself, amazed, *but a few hours ago I fantasized something similar to this and gave myself completion. Now here I am, doing it in reality. Surely the goddess is kind.*

Yet privately, she knew this felt a hundred times better than her fantasy. Gregor's tongue was firm, rough and undeniably real, not some fantasy she had concocted in her mind. His face was not just a shadowy dream, but hovered just a few inches from her pussy, etched into her memory as one of the most beautiful sights she had ever seen.

She could feel the heat of the wall behind her and feel the trembling ache in every straining muscle. All the factors jumbled together until she knew she would remember this moment, no matter what the future held, until her dying day.

Lani caught her breath and watched as Gregor gently bit down onto her clit. Sometime during her musings he had introduced a third finger inside her, and she thought she surely must be stretched to her limit.

Dimly, she realized that just as three of his fingers were curved and fluted inside her, a few fingers of his other hand still toyed playfully with her outer lips. She could feel their slick rubbing on her sensitive flesh. The fingers were well coated with her own juices. This knowledge made her heart beat faster as well.

Gregor pulled his head away to look up into her face. Lani could feel it flush, both with the heat of the room as well as sexual desire. She smiled at him, breathless and unable to convey her desire and happiness any other way.

"Have you fantasized about this, Lani?" he asked darkly, his voice husky with is own need.

"Of course," she replied, breathless and unable to articulate herself any further.

"Then I bet you've also fantasized about *this*," he continued, a knowing gleam in his eye.

Sensitive as she was, Lani nearly bolted from the wall in the small chamber as one of his slick fingers, greased from her own juices gently circled the opening of her back passage. Lani vaguely heard strangled gasping sounds, didn't even really recognize them as coming from her own mouth and throat.

Certainly, in the dark of night, before she decided to join the Force, when she had been trailing around on one starship after another, she had often wondered what anal penetration would be like.

She had been so lonely, even with all the other crew members on board. Everyone had been friendly enough to the new recruit, yet Lani had learned the hard way she didn't belong traveling around the stars and different universes.

Late at night, she had discovered herself, learned her likes and dislikes. And she had fantasized. Fantasized about a dark and handsome lover who would help her discover even more about herself.

Lani smiled. Gregor certainly fit the category of dark, though not in the looks department with his light skin and blond hair. Looking down into storm-tossed gray eyes, Lani knew this was the lover she had dreamed of every night for those years she had felt trapped in her own small world and work.

"I can see it in your eyes, Lani. The desire, the darkest hunger. No man has ever done this, has he?"

Mute, Lani shook her head. Her throat felt parched, despite the wet heat of the chamber. Desire had dried it out better than the desert heat.

"We're going to go on that discovery, Lani. Not tonight, I don't have the time or the patience to give that to you tonight. But soon, little girl, very soon. We're going to explore this and everything else we've both been craving."

With that, Lani felt his slick, thick finger press into her up to the first knuckle. She moaned in painful pleasure. The small finger, even richly wet with her pleasure juices, surely had to be three times larger and thicker than it should be.

Even as she thought this, she knew his finger couldn't possibly be any thicker simply because it was inside her tight, virgin opening. Gregor uttered a hoarse groan and pressed his face into her pussy, lapping and stroking her with twice the vigor of before.

Yet again, he laved and nibbled on her clit. The explosion began deeply inside herself. His finger in her hidden passage stroking the tender, virgin walls, three of his thick fingers inside her and his mouth on her clit, she simply couldn't hold herself back anymore. With the tender, yet sharp, pressure of his teeth against her swollen clit, Lani knew she had just reached her limit.

She felt the whirling mass of emotions and need swirling inside grow and swell. She knew she couldn't hold out any longer. As Gregor laved the swollen bud with his tongue and let his thick finger stroke the inside walls of her back entrance, Lani hit critical mass.

Blindly reaching out, she grabbed either side of Gregor's face with her hands, pulling him away from her oversensitive clit.

"I..." she tried to speak, tried to explain she wanted this to last forever. A part of her knew she had already reached the pinnacle and there would be no turning back, yet still she wanted to cling to the sensations for the rest of her life.

"I..." she tried again, only to feel her eyes cross with the rush of feelings and desires.

Gregor seemed to smile like a satisfied cat. He pressed his finger one knuckle deeper into her back entrance, stroking her and building the desperation of her need to a level she could not contain. Lani could hear buzzing in her ears as her body ripped itself apart with the force of her climax.

She couldn't hold back any longer, her back arched, her head and shoulders pressed into the wall with such pressure she briefly wondered if she would bruise. With three of his fingers still deeply embedded inside her and stroking the tight inner walls of her pussy, Lani felt her inside muscles grasp down and clamp on his digits.

The contractions and climax roared through her, a buzzing, hazy sound rumbling in her ears. For a nanosecond, Lani wondered if she were about to pass out.

Her knees were wobbly, and were it not for the bulk of Gregor's body pressing against them and holding her hips steady with the pressure of his shoulders, she was certain she would have collapsed like the worst sort of old-style heroine in an ungainly heap onto the floor of the chamber.

Slowly her hearing returned, and Lani looked down at her lover. She didn't recall when the water had stopped running and the steam released. The temperature was still warm and cozy, so maybe she hadn't cared enough to worry about the lack of water.

Gregor slowly, gently removed his fingers from her body, sucking wickedly at the three that had been lodged inside her pussy. With his eyes dancing merrily, he easily pushed himself upright and held her steadily in his warm embrace. He nuzzled her neck and she felt more relaxed, more content than she ever recalled feeling.

"You have a knack for that," she croaked, surprised to find her voice not working properly.

"You rather blew me away with your skills, yourself, little girl. I merely returned the favor."

Lani smiled and pushed them both away from the chamber wall. Anticipating her, Gregor opened the door and gallantly held it for her to exit. Letting the room dry her automatically, Lani enjoyed the warm pulses of air, tempted to sit on the floor and let them run seductively over her clit and throbbing labia.

That, however, would be greedy. And she didn't feel certain her emotions were *quite* ready to expose that much of her decadent nature to him just yet. Sure, in the privacy of her own lodgings she might act the hedonistic escort, or sex slave, willing and ready to indulge herself in every conceivable physical delight. Yet that stood as a private side to her, a secret, delectable indulgence.

Dry within the minute, Lani pulled on the robe Gregor handed her and stepped out into the room. Gently, he exerted the slightest amount of pressure onto her arm and led her to the room across the hall. Opening the door, he waved her inside.

"This is your room for what's left of the night."

Lani faced him, a frown marring her face. Remembrance cleared her mind, however.

"Still determined we sleep separately?" she teased him. In truth she would happily spend the next day exploring his body and her own desire.

She had a vivid mental flash where she had him tied to the bed as she made him her sexual slave. All that gloriously naked flesh bound and spread for her personal use...but she pushed that to the very back of her mind.

No sense in getting herself wound up for nothing.

Crossing over to him, rising up on tiptoes, Lani planted a chaste, almost sisterly kiss on his lips. No tongue, no lingering.

"Good night then. Don't forget to wake me up when it's time to go. I'm already packed so it will only take me a few minutes to get ready."

Amused to see a flush of what she now knew enough about him to read as sexual wanting cross his skin, Lani watched him straighten his back and head into his own room and shut the door.

Closing her own door behind her, Lani removed the robe and crawled into the large bed, trying to let her mind relax. This proved exceedingly difficult as snatches of the acts in the cleansing chamber wafted through her conscious. Fiercely, she grabbed hold of her runaway thoughts and tried to rest.

Instead, she recalled the highly erotic paintings gracing the main room in the house, a series of three scenes. She had been astounded by the explicit nature of the scenes, but also surprised by the fierceness of her own reaction to them. They had seared her memory and imprinted themselves onto her brain for a later perusal.

The first scene had been of an open forest glen. The dark brown and green of the trees and grass gave it the earthy feel, a sensual feel of safe forest and damp earth beneath one's feet.

A mythical satyr—half goat, half man—stood behind a woman, both of them in profile to the viewer, locked in the most intimate embrace. The woman looked small, petite, next to the earthy musculature of the satyr.

The satyr clasped the woman's hips, drawing her bottom back, leaning her entire weight onto his hips. Her hands were cupping her own breasts, pinching her own nipples as she arched her back in obvious pleasure.

The satyr had his head buried in the arch of her neck, nipping it, his flash of white teeth erotic against her pale flesh and his own much darker skin. The more Lani had looked at that first painting, the more she had seen.

The satyr had his thick shaft penetrating the woodland nymph, right up her ass, not her pussy as she had first assumed. They had been locked together, completely unaware of anything else in the forest except the culmination of their own pleasure.

Both the satyr and the nymph had been climbing toward ecstasy, and they were almost at their peak if the strain in their postures and the arching of their bodies had been any indication.

It was only as Lani's eyes roved away from the straining, erotic couple she had noticed she was not their only voyeur into their passion.

Other small creatures watched, enthralled, from around the trees and shrubs in the glade. Small gnomes, fairies, other men and women were hazy, shadowy presences throughout the painting. Many of the other voyeurs had been so hazy and deeply hidden in the shadows, they might have been her imagination, or a trick of the light. The sun only shone down on the satyr and his nymph, creating an interesting mixture of light and shadows.

Enthralled, unbelievably turned on, Lani had moved to the second painting. This scene was set under the ocean. A strong merman clasped a mermaid closely to him. The artist had shown the merman face-on, looking hungrily down at his chosen lover.

The man had pale blue skin, and darker blue-green hair, the scales of his tail twinkled brightly in the light under the sea. The mermaid had her head thrown back in ecstasy, she seemed to be on the verge of climax. As Lani recognized this she looked again at the merman. His dark, hungry look also seemed to be filled with masculine satisfaction, and that strained, holding quality she had seen previously in Gregor.

The merman waited for his mate to come before he released himself.

Unlike the woodland scene, this painting seemed focused purely on the merman and mermaid's pleasure. The fact they were set under the sea seemed an unimportant fact to the intensity of the pleasure they shared.

The mermaid's back arched backward, giving the viewer some indication of the beauty of her face, of her long, navy blue tresses as they floated around her in the water. Her eyes were squeezed tightly shut, on the brink of orgasm.

Heart pounding, pussy dampening, Lani had moved to the final scene.

Her breath had caught, her eyes roving the scene before her, wanting to catalogue and ingrain every detail in her mind.

A dark, gray-black storm cloud sat upon the bottom of the scene, instantly creating an unearthly setting. Yet in the far distant corner, tiny beams of perfect, golden sunlight shone through the dark clouds.

In the very center of these clouds, in profile to the viewer, lay an angel. Her shoulder-length blonde hair softly framed her face. She half-sat, half-lay on the dark cloud, her back slightly raised as her arms clasped her lover tightly.

Pure, perfectly white wings sprung from her back. She lay completely naked, unaffected by what had to be a chill wind on the dark, stormy cloud. Her legs were spread and she welcomed her lover, clasped him close to her body.

Her lover had dark blond hair, and a perfectly muscled body. He rested between her legs, one arm keeping them spread to his liking. The other clasped one of her bountiful breasts, tweaking the nipple. There, in front of the goddess and anyone who cared to watch, they coupled.

Fiercely, lovingly but their coupling almost appeared to be rough, from the way they strained against each other. It certainly looked like one of the most erotic scenes Lani had ever witnessed, yet one of the tenderest, one of the most loving and elemental she had ever had the pleasure of viewing.

Now, tucked into bed, Lani felt the ache inside her chest and her womb. Those scenes might have been highly erotic, but they were romantic and climatic as well. They showed a different side to Gregor she had never thought to witness.

They showed he not only had a soul filled with passion and romance, but he yearned for that "something more" she herself had spent many years searching for.

With that thought and a sated smile on her face, she let herself drift into a deep sleep, filled with myriad images and erotic wishes.

Chapter Six
Planet Xylone

ဢ

Leif tightened his hold on the bamboo stalks that made up his headboard. While his wrists were certainly bound around the stalks, he exerted his own pressure, squeezing the stalks as he neared yet another climax.

Sarha, he knew for almost certain, had spent the last day or so trying her level best to make him lose his mind. She currently suckled his sac in her mouth, gently teased him as she rolled both balls encased within it around the heated damp recess of her mouth.

The gentle caresses, the laving of her tongue, the little noises of pleasure she made in the back of her throat made him want to blow his mind and scream his release.

What seemed like hours ago, or maybe it was yesterday, Sarha had told him she wanted to know how much teasing he could, as a man, stand before he blew his load.

She had bound his hands, and started to caress his body. Leif had been astounded at how many ways a woman could touch, stroke, caress, lick and just generally drive a man batty.

Sometime later, but still a fuzzy age ago, Sarha had licked his ear and whispered to him, "When you feel you have reached your end, you must declare 'Yield' to me. But be warned, my Leif, you must not climax before you yield. You must understand the importance of giving everything over to a woman."

Leif had blustered, saying he would *never* come before he could give Sarha her own satisfaction. The young woman had merely smiled her response. During the intervening hours they had talked to each other.

Sarha was twenty years of age, and had been born and raised in the tribe. He had felt an astounding and indescribable joy within himself when she had confessed to him he was her first man.

She had admitted she had broken her own hymen in the ancient tradition on the last full moon. While many women had felt themselves ready to come into their maturity at younger ages, Sarha wanted to learn more of herself, before she made her own decision to prepare to share her burgeoning sexuality with a man.

Smooth wooden phallus-like objects were used by many of the tribeswomen between capturing men. Sarha had eagerly told him how she had gone out hunting and found her own tree, her own piece of wood and carefully, traditionally made her own phallus.

Leif had to exert tremendous control not to shoot his seed everywhere as she had eagerly but self-consciously told her story of her own personal self-discovery. She had been trained in the arts of pleasure-making, knew a million different ways to make a man lose his seed.

Yet she had also shyly confided to him how wrapped up in all that training had been an incredible amount of her own sexual learning. Sarha had explained that by learning what gave herself pleasure, it helped her understand how to return the same excitement and fulfillment to a man.

Leif was amazed at how basic and integral the Amazon's main philosophy was. Bringing one's partner pleasure was only one of the most important aspects of sex and sharing one's body. Helping bring about their *own* physical pleasure lay intimately wrapped up in it as well.

It all seemed so simple he couldn't understand why all sexual congress classes didn't explain it like this. By learning about your own sexuality, sexual needs and desires, one became a better lover.

Leif moaned.

"Sarha, you need to let me help pleasure you. I don't want to come alone. I want to bring you the same pleasure you've brought me."

"My Leif, learning to accept pleasure is just as important as giving it."

Leif smiled wryly at Sarha's comment. He could taste the truth in it, but that didn't make it any easier to accept.

"Sarha," he croaked, and then tried to swallow and get some moisture in his mouth. He knew he couldn't last much longer, he could feel the massive climax build in his balls. "Sarha, I love what you're doing to me, and trust me, babe, you can do this to me anytime. I just want to give you some pleasure as well. I *need* to give you pleasure as well. Please."

Leif was astounded as Sarha stopped licking and caressing his staff and sac, raised her body so her breasts crushed into his chest. Deftly, she unbound his hands. Wincing at the slight pain as the blood circulated more freely into them, Leif shook his arms and hands.

"Did I bind them too tightly?" Sarha worried, gnawing on her lower lip.

Leif rolled them both over, so his straining erection pressed into her soft belly. Crushing her breasts into his chest, loving the feel of her underneath him, he smiled a rakish, delighted smile.

"Not at all, they just have a bit of stiffness in them from being held in the one spot so long. Don't worry, babe."

The bright, happy, relieved smile Sarha graced him with made his heart pound faster. Her blonde hair spilled out around the cushions and silks over her bed. The most amazing, beautiful sea-green eyes stared up into his, and he could feel his heart slipping out of his grasp and into her strong one.

Bending his head down, he kissed her, softly, gently. He knew for all her exalted *self-discovery* it happened to be impossible to kiss oneself. And practicing on one's own hand and arm simply could not compete.

At one stage, he had asked if she had practiced a time or two on her female tribe mates. He had been charmed and amazed at the fiery red blush that had covered her face and neck.

"A time or two," she had admitted hesitantly, "but while I did not mind it as such, I did not find it particularly enjoyable either."

Just the mental image of his Sarha prettily practicing kissing another of her tribe mates was enough for his painfully erect cock to twinge in desire. And so he had decided it was his manly duty to give her as much lips-on-lips practice at kissing as possible.

Not that he felt this was a chore. In point of fact he knew he would self-combust if he wasn't constantly given the opportunity to press his lips against her much softer ones.

As he reached one tingling hand up to cup her beautiful breast, to feel the rasp of erect nipple against his tender palm, he remembered the vid they had seen during their sexual congress classes back in their final year at age sixteen.

"Foreplay is most important for any female. Studies have shown the longer time spent in foreplay, the more enjoyable congress becomes for the woman. Also, it makes it far easier for the man to penetrate her, as she is richly wet with her own lubricant."

Leif smiled as he reached his other hand down to her nether lips. As the vid had promised, Sarha was moist and wet with her own fluids. Swirling a finger about her slick outer lips, he raised his hand and, while he looked deeply into her sea-green eyes, placed one finger inside his mouth, sucking hungrily on her juices.

Tasting the salty, feminine cream he knew he would always remember this woman and this time.

"I've got the taste of you now, Sarha. Cream will never taste so good again."

Sarha blushed again, and reached her own hand down to fist his engorged shaft. Pumping him, Leif could feel the last threads of his control begin to fray.

"This first time might not be as slow as you want, babe," he warned, rolling them again on the large bed so she straddled him in the age-old position of female dominance.

Sarha rose to the challenge, resting both her hands on his chest, toying with his nipples, which he was astonished at how sensitive they were. He had heard in congress class women's nipples were extraordinarily sensitive, but nowhere had he ever heard male nipples were also sensitive to touch during sex.

"I want you hot and hard and right now, Leif. We can go much slower the second time. Witch Doctor told us that you were young enough and hot enough to rise many times during the one night. I would like this to be hard and hot and rough, this first time we share together."

Moaning, her words firing him beyond his control and patience, Leif reached down to align her hips with his cock. Gently spreading her lower lips wide, he softly, carefully penetrated her for the first time. He adored the sound of her moan, drank it deep within his soul and held it close as one of his best memories.

Finally, after what he felt certain was an age of gently pressing forward, toying with her nipples and labia and then pressing more, they lay skin to skin, completely joined and achingly full.

Leif had never known such pleasure and encompassing heat. It was as if he knew everything, as if he could discover anything, as if he could solve the galaxy's problems, right every wrong and conquer the known universe.

He felt like the king of the world.

Sarha moaned and dug her short nails into his chest. The pain she gave to him was exquisite, the perfect counterpoint to the incredible pleasure of their union. As they gathered their breath, Sarha began to move.

Slowly, she lifted herself up, raising her body so the friction of her pussy being removed from his cock sent shivers down both their spines. Leif had never experienced anything like the hammering pleasure from within his cock and all through his chest.

The tiny pricks of her nails against his chest seemed to somehow highlight the sucking, pressured pleasure encompassing his cock.

Leif groaned, feeling the gloving heat leave his cock. Gritting his teeth, he knew he shouldn't grab her hips to bring her back down, though the temptation to do so was unbelievably powerful.

Sarha waited a moment, paused with her slit just above the tip of his erection, and then sank back down on him. The incredibly tight, warm feeling had them both crying out with the electric sensation of her clasping him so tightly once more.

Over and over Sarha withdrew and then came back, withdrew and came back. Leif thought his mind would explode with the incredible desire.

"Sarha, you have to do something, I need to come really badly."

The woman above him merely smiled in that secret, utterly catlike way women across the galaxy had. Returning the smile, purely masculine and definitely hungry, Leif grabbed her shoulders, pulled her toward him and kissed her hungrily.

Loving the taste of her mouth, the softness of her lips, he lingered a moment, and then gently rolled them over yet again.

This time *he* had the control. Holding her hips steady, he withdrew and plunged into her, over and over. He urgently needed the feel of her clasping at him, embracing him.

He could feel them both reaching up, striving for that climax. He had heard it described to him, yet never had he truly understood how one could feel themselves and their chosen partner striving for that elusive peak.

Pumping ferociously into her now, holding her steady and loving how open and trusting Sarha was, how she matched him step for step, Leif cried out as he sensed his climax overtaking him.

Just before he started to erupt, Sarha took one of his hands, and brought it to the apex of her slit.

"Rub here," she insisted, gasping and straining. Leif touched the warm bud, a small, erect piece of flesh. With his thumb he rubbed it, not fully understanding, but willing to do absolutely anything she asked of him.

He could feel Sarha quiver and gasp underneath him, and so he rubbed even harder, circling his finger around the strange nub.

And then the light dawned.

"Your clit?" he gasped in query. He had heard the piece of anatomy mentioned, but hadn't really been paying attention, too focused on the full frontal nude picture of a woman to want to listen to his instructor.

Sarha only nodded, and convulsed around him. The tight squeezing of her pussy drove every thought from his mind. He would later swear that it was as if his balls and cock had exploded, as if the top of his head blew off his shoulders.

He dimly realized his cock spurted jet after jet of seed into his woman, emptying himself and draining him of all his energy simultaneously.

A moment later, he collapsed nearly on top of her, remembering at the last moment to fall aside so as to not crush her. He was winded, wrung utterly dry. Almost as if he had run a marathon or swum across the ocean. Never had he felt such utter, encompassing exhaustion.

"That... That was... Sarha, I've never had such utter fantastic sex."

"Of course not," she replied smugly, reaching down to cover them. "You were a virgin. I think you have brilliant potential though."

Gaping, Leif wondered how she knew.

"The Witch Doctor warned me it could be so. But you didn't need any help. I bet you've had teachings too, right?"

Smiling at the cheeky woman grinning across at him, he embraced her and turned her so they became spooned.

"I think we should catch a quick nap. I'll show you what I've learned when we awaken. Sound fair?"

"Definitely," she murmured, "but I might show you a few of my own tricks too."

"I'll look forward to it," he whispered in her ear, snuggling down for a much-needed snooze.

Chapter Seven

ॐ

The man sat at his personal computer, tapping his fingers impatiently while he waited for his comm to arrive. He had been so careful with his plans, had been patient for months after his beloved Uncle's death while he spun the complex web now about to be laid out.

All he needed was this final missive to inform him the game had started.

Revenge seemed to be the best motivator in the galaxy. His half-brother had been slain, the grief of this causing the untimely death of their Uncle, and the man's thirst for revenge had only grown over the months.

The official inquiry his Uncle, bedridden and steadily growing weaker by the hour, had insisted on had only brought back results of "...the wrong place at the wrong time," and "In the confusion of the insurgence..."

The man had been deep in hiding so he had not received word of what he deep in his soul knew could only have been his half-brother's murder, until his Uncle had finally given up his tenuous hold on life.

The man knew he could never rest until his revenge for his slain half-brother, as well as the resulting death of his Uncle, had been completed.

So deeply hidden had the man been, his Uncle had died soon after the report had been given to him, thinking his last two living relations were also dead.

The resulting guilt had spurred the man on with his plans for revenge as much as his anger at the murders itself. The mixture of guilt and anger proved to the man he had to kill everyone involved in the underhand plot that had caused such mayhem in his life.

Weeks of searching, hacking and calling in every favor owed to him had finally brought back some results. He had found the names of the three people responsible for his half-brother's death, and thus also responsible for his Uncle's death.

The man tapped his fingers impatiently, waiting for his minion's report that the first part of his plan was in action.

The man smiled his evil smile as he wondered at the vagrancies of Fate and the galaxy. What had begun as a quest for power, as an idle wish to rule the greater half of the galaxy, had quickly become a quest to ruin the two men and the one woman who were responsible for changing his life as no one previously had ever done.

The man had not been dismayed or upset in the slightest when one of those two men had begun to cover his tracks, to protect himself and the woman, now his new Bondmate.

For those actions simply left the second man, far more cocky and arrogant in his single state. And so, contrary to his initial plans, it would be the second man they were laying the trap for. And who would, undoubtedly, be the one to help him reel in the other man and woman.

Once the man, and maybe even his minion if he survived, had captured their conceited quarry, they could reveal the rest of their plans for vengeance.

But first, the man must wait by his comm, telling himself that all had been lain out as structured in his plan.

Frustrated, but unwilling to move from his comfortable chair, the man stared out the window into the jungle beyond. Wildly colored plants and vegetation grew mere feet from his bungalow and window. Colors he hadn't even known existed just a few months ago sprouted from the ground and the vines which surrounded the small hut he currently resided in.

Tapping his fingers, still impatient, the man mentally ran over his plans, over his trap yet again. He could find no holes, could detect no weaknesses anywhere in his careful scheme. Smiling smugly, he sat back, knowing his will would prevail.

Just as he had planned, his personal comm unit beeped the incoming message. Finally able to relax, he poured himself a drink and slowly began to sip it. Once the message fully downloaded, he read it and smiled again.

The web is set and the boy taken, but the blowfly was executed. The game is afoot. Your Minion.

The man raised his glass in a silent toast to acknowledge his own genius. Everything would follow his plan and his revenge would be perfected. All he needed to do now would be to sit and wait for the events to unfold around him.

More often than not, he had found, great men's plans failed when they became too eager, too restless and tampered with their own greatness.

The man had no plans to do that. He would wait patiently and let all his little flies become entangled all by themselves. Then he would come in, the big, bad spider, and gobble them all up.

The man sat smugly, sipping his drink, watching the jungle outside. He had learned patience many, many years ago at a hard school.

Soon his revenge would be complete.

Chapter Eight

$\wp$

Lani slowly became aware of her mind sluggishly trying to sort out the myriad different, equally magnificent sensations stringing through her body. Nerve endings blazed a heated trail of erotic sensations. Hot breath puffed over her sensitized skin, warmer than any caress in her life.

A rough, rasping tongue slid slick and warm over the main pulse point in her neck.

Lani moaned, unable to help herself. She turned fully onto her back and arched her neck to allow better access for the tongue that played over her skin and the heated palm that slid down her body.

Her mind still foggy with sleep, Lani gasped at the sensations coursing through her body. Her skin burned with erotic fire where the wet tongue trailed languidly along its path. Her torso leaped to life and craved the attention of the hand wandering over it.

"Please," she begged, not even certain exactly what it was she craved or pleaded for.

"Wake up, Lani," a familiar, husky voice whispered over her skin.

Wanting more, more of everything, his tongue, his touch, his caress and his heat, Lani begged again for the first time in her life.

"Please," she replied, reaching up blindly to the head nestled in the arch of her shoulder. Pulling him up, she eagerly sought his lips with her own. Not even giving him time to resist her, she crushed her lips to his. Slanting her mouth, she deepened the kiss, sliding her tongue between his surprised lips.

He tasted hot and salty, masculine and spicy. The smoothness of his hair, the short silky strands, confirmed the reality of her dream. Gregor lay in her—his—bed and she shuddered with the erotic sensations as her body tightened and the heat within her grew fourfold.

She penetrated his mouth with her tongue as she *craved* his cock to penetrate her folds. Yet she knew she only had a moment or two.

Recklessly, uncaring of the repercussions, she dipped one hand down to his crotch. Annoyed, she discovered him already dressed in his skinsuit.

This would prove harder than she originally thought.

At the heat radiating from the strong erection under its suit and her hand, Lani smiled for the first time that morning. *Hard* wouldn't be a word she wanted to think too deeply about.

Hoping for something, any sort of satisfaction, she stroked her "partner" through his pants. His low moan satisfied at least one curiosity. He wanted her as much, if not more, than she wanted him.

"Lani," he panted. She ignored him and continued to both kiss and stroke him. "Lani," he growled, louder and stronger.

Lani rolled them both on the big bed, moaning when their lips broke contact. With Gregor on his back, Lani finally opened her eyes. The room was still shrouded in darkness, though the beginning stages of dawn let a small chink of light in.

Lani straddled Gregor's hips, loving the thick, hard muscles that fairly vibrated with his desire for her.

Pressing her mound down, she had to bite her lip not to moan her desire to shred his suit from his body. With only her bare flesh, she could easily feel his heat radiating through her skin, heating her deeply within.

If only he weren't wearing his suit she could... She cut off that train of thought before she really did drive herself wild.

Her hands grasping his shoulders, she bent down to kiss him once more. In about five seconds he would realize she wasn't asleep, and she doubted he would let her burn off some of this fire raging inside her body.

She wanted to ride him, wild and free, more than she wanted her next deep breath. She wanted to strip him completely naked, lick and touch every inch of his delectable skin and sate herself for the next dozen hours or so.

Instead, they had to board a starship and rescue her stupid godson from whatever scrape he had managed to make for himself. Taking a deep breath, she inhaled the spicy fragrance Gregor had used when he removed his beard earlier. His hot hands grabbed her hips and for one delicious moment, ground her farther down onto his straining erection.

And then sanity returned.

Gregor neatly, and with a casual ease that had her grinding her teeth, flipped them both again on the bed, so he ground down into her. If only he weren't in that damned skinsuit...

"This," he huskily murmured into her ear, causing her nerve endings to zing and her breath to become choppy, "is your wake-up call. You have five minutes to dress and pack and be ready to leave for the ship."

Refusing to be passive at this late stage, Lani moved her hands and pulled him down so their lips fused again. The eagerness with which he kissed her, the fierce abandon and desire pouring through the kiss to singe her to her very soul, convinced her he wanted her just as much as she desired him.

Imprinting herself on him, wanting him to feel her long after she had moved away, Lani poured all her desire and heat and need into the last kiss. Even though he kissed her back just as fiercely, Lani knew she would have to seduce him, would have to work out some plan to overcome his resistance.

Finally, breaking the kiss and gasping for air, Lani pulled away.

As the first rays of dawn came in through the window, Lani stared into Gregor's silvery eyes. A deep, dark heat dwelled within there.

Oh yeah, she confirmed silently to herself, *he desired her*. Yet for some reason she could not fathom the hungry beast within him remained leashed.

A part of her knew he wanted to head on out to the trip, but another part of her wondered if maybe he wanted to draw out this game of cat-and-mouse, just to heighten the already astonishing levels of sexual tension between them.

He grinned at her, his eyes crinkled with the laughter.

"Now *that* was some wake-up call. If I hadn't already been dressed..."

Lani smiled, refusing to back down.

"If you hadn't been dressed, we could have had a whole lot more fun." Running her hand through his hair again, loving the silky texture and feel of it between her fingers, Lani bent upward once more, unable to help herself.

Giving him a perfectly chaste kiss, a gentle press of lips on lips, she pulled away before she really *did* just strip his suit from him and ride his cock until they both exploded.

Instead, she pulled herself upright and swung her legs from the bed.

"I am assuming it's almost time we head for the port?"

Gregor merely nodded, his eyes feasting on her body. Lani smiled, taunted him as she stood naked in front of the dawning sunlight.

"I know you want me, Gregor. And I'm more than certain you know I want you just as much. I've just decided I'm going to seduce you. I think it's good of me to warn you up front, whenever I decide things like this, I never stop until I have what I want."

"Good?" he queried, a deep hunger lighting his eyes.

"Yeah," she purred as she stepped toward him, towering over him on the bed. "I don't like to take advantage. I want you to know full well what I intend. I've wanted you for weeks. Neither of us is on official assignment. I think this is the perfect time for, what did they used to call it? A holiday fling?"

Gregor smiled. "And what about when the holiday is over?"

Lani shrugged, unwilling to commit any further. More than likely he would have grown weary of her by the time they headed back home. The only consistency Lani had gleaned from gossip was Gregor's flings were always brief. If she were to stay in control of this thing, she would need to make sure they broke up before he grew bored.

"When the holiday's over undoubtedly we'll both go back to work, and be back under the Force's regs. Why, you complaining?" she teased him, knowing no man would give up no-strings-attached sex.

Surprisingly, Gregor merely looked directly into her eyes. Lani tried to suppress the shiver that washed through her. The intensity of his gaze made her wonder if he could see straight through to her very soul.

She had the uncomfortable feeling for a fleeting moment that he could see her every fantasy and wish. Lani knew it was impossible, but as those quicksilver eyes scanned her slowly and methodically, he seemed to penetrate to her very heart and soul.

When Gregor broke their eye contact he pushed himself up from the bed. Before she could stop or help herself, she took a step backward.

Gregor snaked a hand out, cupping her face and bringing her closer to him. He angled himself perfectly, without thought, and kissed her passionately. When he pulled away, Lani could swear she had no breath in her lungs. Gasping like a virgin, she stared up into his eyes.

"I think," he started huskily, "this will be the most interesting trip I've made in years. You can lead for now, Lani, but I will warn you. When the time comes, I do believe I will take great joy in completely taking over."

Lani smiled, enjoying his taunts. "I don't know, Gregor, a big strong man like you? I think you're begging for a woman to take control of *you* and—" She squealed and ducked the strong arm that snaked out to grab her, Lani laughed as she danced away.

Until she bumped up against the window.

In an instant Gregor was there, hot and hard, pressing her softer body back against the warm glass.

"I think you're begging for a Mastering, Lani. You poke and prod at my control as if you want nothing more than for me to snap and dominate you. But for now, I'm happy to move at your pace. Never let it be said that I wouldn't follow a woman's games and see her happy. Now, get dressed and meet me downstairs. We have a starship to catch."

With a hot, hard kiss, he left the room with Lani's knees melting and her lungs gasping for air. Sure, she wanted to push his buttons, but something feminine deep inside warned her against pushing him too far.

Smiling, completely ignoring her own internal warning system, Lani quickly changed into her own skinsuit and grabbed her few belongings. She had never been dominated before, never experienced this wicked thrill of adrenaline or excitement at the mere thought of a man taking full control of their lovemaking.

Running a brush through her hair and pulling it back into a ponytail, she walked out of her door less than five minutes later. While her knees still wobbled and her heart still pounded, she was more in control of herself and her reckless emotions now.

She might indeed let Gregor take control of their lovemaking.

But it would be on her terms.

Smiling, looking forward to the next couple of days, Lani slung her bag over her shoulder. A small part of her brain insisted she should be worried about Leif, should be making him her top priority. She had pushed the grief over losing her two dearest friends to the back of her mind. Her grieving would have to come later. Lani knew Amazons had never seriously hurt any man in their keeping. The worst thing that could happen to her godson would be sexual exhaustion.

Lani tried to swallow a giggle as she headed toward Gregor. She honestly couldn't remember the last time she had giggled like a schoolgirl.

Sexual exhaustion? She almost envied Leif.

She should be so lucky!

Chapter Nine

හ

Gregor drank his glass of vitawater down and tried to rein in his wayward emotions and out-of-control body. How could one small woman undo him so easily?

So lost had he become in his thoughts, he realized he had been staring stupidly at his empty glass for a few moments. When had he finished it? He wondered if he should drink another one down, just to be sure.

One glass of vitawater supposedly fueled the body with enough vitamins and minerals to keep a person healthy for the entire day. But as Gregor couldn't even remember drinking it down, he figured it couldn't hurt to have another.

Quickly refilling the glass, he lifted it to his lips only to promptly choke as Lani entered the small kitchen area.

The casual ease with which she smiled at him and poured herself her own glass of the liquid damn near had him drooling at the thought of stripping them both bare and allowing himself permission to touch her body. Every curve, every crevice...

"I'm ready. You're just taking that small bag?" she commented idly as she nodded to his small sack. Actually, Gregor grinned to himself, the sack contained a hell of a lot of things. It was a pack-all-sack, and its small size was incredibly deceiving, but who was he to burst her bubble?

"Yep. Drink that down and we can head on out," he commented curtly.

Gregor mentally cursed his body and its incredible reaction to the luscious lady in front of him. How the hell could he run this rescue mission with a woman he wanted to fuck in every conceivable position with every breath he drew?

On top of that, how could he continue to be kissing her wildly one minute, and then issuing curt orders the next? Most women wouldn't stand for it, but Lani seemed to almost understand his wildly fluctuating emotions. Which gave her even more power and made him feel even more confused about their unique situation.

Get a bloody grip on yourself, he chided, mentally running through his checklist. Somehow, some way he had to regain control of himself and this mission. He could feel himself losing control to Lani and they hadn't even left his lodgings yet.

As Lani carefully placed her empty glass down on the counter, he rinsed it and left it beside his own for the washer to clean and place back in its designated spot. Slinging his bag over his shoulder, he indicated with a nod of his head for Lani to follow him.

Maybe he could speak to her in the Force sign language? At least that way he wouldn't be issuing curt orders, which would eventually upset her feminine sensibilities.

Locking the lodgings up tightly, glad he had the foresight to forewarn the local beat about his absence, he threw both their bags into the backseat of his Cruiser and helped Lani in.

Happy to finally be on their way, he began to relax as the power of his new transport and the ease with which he could control *it* washed over him.

It wasn't until they were nearly at the port he realized they had been sitting in silence almost the entire trip.

"You okay?" he asked idly, turning into the large parking area. Out of the corner of his eye he could see her shrug. Shooting her a quick glance, he concentrated for a moment on parking the Cruiser. Removing his safety belt, he turned to face her fully.

"What is it?"

When Lani faced him, he forced himself to concentrate on her words, and not the insane urge he had to palm her breast,

114

or lick his way down her neck, or… With a great deal of effort, he brought his eyes up to stare into her deep green ones. She smiled at him, almost as if she could read his thoughts.

"I've just been thinking of Leif, wondering if he'll even want me to rescue him. I did an awful lot of research on these Amazons. They don't hurt their captives. More often than not they release them after they tire of them anyway."

"If he doesn't want to be rescued, we can always stay in the vicinity and help him get back home when he's ready. There is also the little matter of the murder of your friends. We can try to get some answers to that while we wait."

Gregor swallowed a groan of lust as she bit down on her full lower lip. He honestly couldn't remember the last time he had wanted a woman so much. At the moment, he thought he might have the upper hand. Sure, he was stiff as an iron rod and felt like he hadn't had relief of any sort in months, but he hadn't yet lost control.

Pulling her over onto his lap and fucking her here in the front area of the transport in full view of anyone who happened to look would definitely constitute losing it.

For a split second, Gregor indulged himself and imagined how it would unfold. Pulling Lani's navy blue skinsuit down, fingering her damp slit, spreading the juices he found there around her clit. Watching her back arch as she began moaning in lust and need.

Gregor could feel the silk of her long blonde hair as it ran through his fingers, could taste her lips as they pressed down on him. Finally, he had to drag his thoughts away as he was coming way too close to climax just from the imaginary feel of himself sliding deeply inside her warm, wet, welcoming pussy.

He could perfectly feel the tightness of her gloving pussy, the sweet friction unlike anything else across the galaxy of a man thrusting inside his woman.

"What is it?" he heard her say. Blinking his eyes, returning to reality, Gregor reached over the back of his seat to grab both their bags.

"Nothing," he said, silently cursing his hoarse voice. He really would need to do something about this infatuation. If he didn't get inside her, and soon, he would likely throw her down and take her at a most inopportune moment.

He smiled cynically at himself. Yeah. Maybe if he could convince himself it would be for the betterment of *the job* he would be able to fuck them both raw and not need to think about the insane desire he was inundated with every single time he looked at or thought about her.

Abstinence was such an unfamiliar thing for him he was utterly surprised by how it made him want to tear something into pieces. He honestly couldn't remember the last time he hadn't tackled a problem head-on and with a logical, cool mind.

His mind shied away from the question of *why* he couldn't think calmly or logically when Lani became involved.

Safeguarding the Cruiser, patting the beautiful girl goodbye, he handed Lani her bag and experienced a measure of relief as they headed into the port.

Outside the close confines of his transport he didn't feel as giddy, or as drunk on her presence. Maybe this whole infatuation thing was actually some alien form of claustrophobia.

The cynical smirk returned to his face. Sure. And maybe he wouldn't need to lose himself in her body or fuck her out of his system at all. Something much bigger than he had ever come across seemed to be happening. All he needed to do would be work out what was occurring and then fix it.

As they neared the area they would use, Gregor's hand twitched with the contact of Lani's skin.

"We're going over here, right?" she asked, touching his arm in the most casual way. The innocent contact nearly broke all his iron-hard control.

"Yep," he grunted, struggling mightily to control himself.

Control? his mind mocked him. *You think you have CONTROL here?*

For the first time, Gregor realized he was in deep shit.

Forcing himself to be calm, he took Lani's arm and guided her to where they needed to be. Pulling a green folder out of his sack, he began the calm, orderly, well-known trade of credits for a ship.

Here, at least, he excelled, totally in his element. He could feel the respect and awe burning into his body as Lani kept her mouth shut and simply smiled at the dealer.

Ten minutes later, he shook hands with the man, and took the cards and the compulsory emergency manual he needed for the starship.

He and Lani boarded and immediately began to work. He noticed Lani seemed amazed and enthralled by everything he did. Feeling much easier, he explained everything as he worked, calmly and step-by-step going through the reasons behind everything he did and what tasks they performed.

In next to no time they were both buckled in and taking off.

Gregor didn't even want to think of how they would pass the time. He'd packed a deck of cards in the sack...hadn't he?

Chapter Ten

ဆ

Lani couldn't help her facial expression of disgust as she nibbled on a spacechocolate bar. When Gregor laughed at her, she reluctantly found a smile crossing her own face.

"Does this stuff always taste so awful?" she couldn't help asking.

"Pretty much," Gregor replied as he seemed to concentrate fully on the controls before him. Lani rolled her eyes. *Men!* She couldn't help but be amused at his singular lack of objection to such a disgusting imitation.

"Chocolate is an institution. This is a hanging offense, this base, crude so-called abomination!" she insisted.

"You're the one who insisted—" Lani cut Gregor off before he could even finish *that* sentence.

"Don't you dare bring this back on me. I asked if you had adequate supplies, and you told me you did." Realizing she sounded like a pouting child, Lani sat back down in her seat and tried to think of a way to change the topic gracefully.

Fiercely taking another bite of the chocolate bar, she stared out the portal into the endless darkness of space.

Gregor continued to click on the control keys, and Lani closed her eyes and took a deep breath.

"I'm sorry," she started, "I am not overly fond of flying in such small ships, even though I know there is absolutely nothing to fear. Eating chocolate is a comfort to me, and concentrating on how disgusting this tastes is better for me than wondering about the science behind how such a small ship can manage to fly through space with nothing but the different forces of gravity to keep it going."

Lani kept on talking while scrutinizing the bar. She turned it over in her hand as she wondered if it would taste better from the other end. It had never seemed to work before, but as her grandmother had used to say, there was always a first time for everything.

Refusing to go down that path and think about *other* firsts she wouldn't mind having with the man sitting in the chair next to her, Lani concentrated purposely and fully on her spacechocolate. So fully had she managed to focus, it came as a surprise when Gregor gently took the bar from her hand and placed it behind him on one of the benches.

She hadn't heard him stand up and for a nanosecond of panic wondered if he shouldn't still be sitting by the controls. What if something happened?

Sanity, however, swiftly returned with the realization he must have put the ship on autopilot.

He stood so closely to her that Lani could feel the heat radiating from his body. Her eyes widened and, trying to regain her earlier calm, she looked behind him to the controls.

"Shouldn't you...?" she trailed off, the expression in his eyes making her mouth dry.

"The ship will take care of itself for a while. So you need a distraction, huh?" Lani swallowed and tried to replace some moisture in her mouth. She could see so many different things in his swirling gray eyes. Hunger. Need. An aching desire to possess her. Everything mixed together until she felt almost snared, captured in the clear, silvery-gray mists.

"Gregor..." she breathed, unsure of exactly what she wanted to say. Before she could even try to organize her thoughts, the warmth of his hands cupped her shoulders. Lani smiled, enjoying the sensation of him exerting a small amount of pressure, and let him help her to her feet.

For a moment, she was unsteady in the pressurized gravity cabin and gasped, wondering if she would fall. The warm pressure remained under her shoulder, keeping her steady, the strength and the heat of his hands counteracting her imbalance.

As if sensing her slight disorientation, he drew her even closer to the heat of his body, stabilizing her.

Without conscious thought, she let her arms creep around his back, to touch and stroke him through the suit. Heat emanated from his body, warming her, branding her.

One of his hands moved up from her shoulder to cup her chin, tilting her face in the manner he wanted. She knew what was about to occur, and she smiled, letting herself relax and enjoy it.

Gregor's face lowered to hers, slowly, so seductively she had to resist the urge to pull him down faster. Finally, after what she felt sure was an age, his lips touched hers. They were soft, warm and strong against hers. Lani let one of her own hands raise up to cup his cheek, to gently pull him closer.

For one beautiful moment, Lani wallowed in the sweet, almost chaste way Gregor kissed her. Such a gentle press of lips against lips. The moment passed and an incredible hunger roared through her, unlike anything she had ever experienced with another man.

It was almost as if an enormous fire shot through her body, so strongly did her desire overtake her. Lani pulled his face closer, and without conscious thought, gently bit down on his lower lip, urging him on.

As if that same fire transferred itself from her to him, Gregor turned her body and pressed her up against the wall, pinning her. His movements seemed reckless, urgent, as if he simply couldn't help himself any longer.

Lani smiled to herself and indulged in the sensation of being branded.

With one of his hands holding her hips steady and the other angling her chin back for his lips to crush against hers, Lani could feel tingling warmth spread through her body. She let herself go lax, as if every muscle had sighed in relief and the tension had simply run away from her.

She smiled as she realized her body had surrendered to Gregor, accepted him. She didn't have to fight herself anymore, and in that realization came a form of freedom and completion, a fulfilling satisfaction.

Lani had by no means lived a chaste life, yet she had never truly managed to fully trust her lovers. She always thought her way through sex. Worries usually rocketed through her mind. *Do I look good from this angle? Does he like me touching him here? Should I rub my own clit to instigate my climax or should I wait for my lover?*

Questions and self-doubt usually tumbled through her head during lovemaking, ruining the effects of her body's release.

Yet this time, knowing Gregor could bring her pleasure, having wanted him for so many weeks and after looking for someone like him for months, she experienced an overwhelming relief as all her doubts, questions and worries simply drained away.

She found odd, new emotions zing through her body, making her strangely exhilarated as the body-sapping weakness and languid excitement overtook her.

Lani let her hand fall down, until they both once again rested against his hips, drawing the heat of his thick cock closer to her aching need.

"I wanted this first time of ours to be slow, Lani. Sweet," he muttered, as he pulled himself away slightly to gasp for breath.

Lani knew deep inside her that Gregor truly did want this to be sweet as she, too, could feel the difference between them. Theirs would not be a one-night stand, or a quick couple of fuckfests. Somehow they both seemed to know what lay between them was different, and she had a feeling they both wanted to start sweet, and then work their way up to the crashing heights they both knew they could reach.

She also knew the fire that raged soul-deep inside both of them wouldn't let all of their lovemaking be that sweet, that gentle. The need inside them burnt too hard, too brightly.

Strangely, now that she was here, and they had found their way to this first moment, instead of wanting this first real time between them to be gentle and sweet, Lani allowed that fire inside her rise to meet Gregor. Lani had had gentle, sweet sex for years, had indulged in the tender lovemaking most men were comfortable with.

One of the first things that had drawn her to Gregor was his innate maleness, an answering heat and darkness within him that she intimately knew and understood. She knew he wouldn't care if they were tender or raw and primal during their sex, he would accept it all. Lani wanted to explore her deeper, darker self with him.

Not wanting to speak, wary of verbalizing her clawing desperate need for him, Lani instead arched herself into him, stripping his suit-shirt from his chest in one rending tear. The sound of the thin fabric ripping seemed loud in the hushed cabin. It seemed so primal, so elemental. Life-changing in a way she couldn't describe.

"Lani—" Gregor choked. Lani could almost feel the fire inside him begin to burn out of control.

Maybe, like the mythical phoenix scientists constantly tried to find and prove, they needed to let themselves be burnt, consumed in the flames of their attractions. Once they both rose from these flames they would know their direction and purpose through this affair.

Besides, Lani couldn't help thinking, *I like the feeling of power he gives me, that the sex between us gives me. I enjoy the sound of his suit tearing and the feel of him beneath my hand. A man wouldn't hesitate to do this, so why the hell should I?*

Quickly, she removed what remained of his suit-shirt, eager to run her hands over his smooth muscles. Lightly tanned, the thin sprinkling of dark blond hair turned her on as little else could. Not even waiting to see what his reaction would be, Lani bent down slightly and ran her mouth over his skin.

She wallowed in her enjoyment of his body. The smooth as silk skin of his chest, the rough hairiness that tickled her lips and nose. She could feel the heat from inside him begin to radiate from his skin. A light, pale red flush began to creep up his chest.

I turn him on! her mind informed her excitedly. *I really, TRULY turn him on!*

This knowledge alone made her want him more. Nothing, to her mind, acted as a more potent aphrodisiac than the knowledge of one's own sexiness. Lani laved her tongue over his nipple, enjoying the masculine scent of him and the faint saltiness of his skin. When he groaned and held her head steady over his nipple, an imp of mischief rose inside her.

Gently, wanting to make him explode with need but not really hurt him in any manner, she bit into the now-sensitive nipple.

"Lani," he panted, no longer Mr. Cool-and-in-control. "I don't think this is helping me to be very gentle."

Lani smiled around his nipple, sucking it into her mouth and drawing on it, just as she loved having done to her. She murmured in her throat, hoping he understood she had no problems with hot and heavy this time around.

Her hands were busy tugging the rest of his ruined suit down over his lean hips. She heard a soft *rip* and she could no more help the chuckle in her throat than she could stop breathing.

"Lani—" Gregor tried again, but she refused to pay attention to him. She was having fun, dammit, and she didn't want to stop anytime soon. Besides, he wriggled his hips, trying to simultaneously get her to suck his nipple harder, thrust his heated cock, even through his thin suit, between her breasts as well as remove his shoes all at once. Lani could just imagine how ridiculous he looked.

Lani's sense of the absurd suddenly reared its head. They must look like a couple of teenagers trying to neck in their parents' ship!

Drawing back, albeit reluctantly, from his large, warm chest, Lani looked up at her man. With a huge grin, she caught his eye. With a vehemence she hadn't realized he'd been struggling with, he pulled one boot off, throwing it to the other side of the cabin.

The other boot followed with lightning speed.

Standing there, with his suit-shirt in tatters around his ankles, and his pants down at his knees, Lani couldn't help but laugh. She laughed loud and long as she hadn't been able to in more years than she could count. Her knees wobbled and she had to slide down the wall until she crouched on her haunches.

After a moment or two, her laughter turned into a few chuckling hiccups, and then finally subsided.

Catching her breath, still sitting back on her haunches, she finally took a deep breath. She smiled and looked up at Gregor. Slowly, she wriggled out of her skinsuit, wanting to be naked like him too much to try and draw out the moment.

"You know, the thought just struck me..." she trailed off as she removed the last of the thin suit, dropping it carelessly onto the floor. She smiled, wondered if Gregor would appreciate the same brand of humor as herself.

"That we're going at it like a couple of sex-starved teens just past their eighteenth majority?" he finished, for her, a wicked, mischievous light in his eyes. "Let me guess," he continued as he crouched down onto his hands and knees.

The very strong image of a hungry, feral golden tiger from the Ancient China flashed through her mind. With his tanned skin, dark blond hair, storm-gray eyes and strongly muscled body, he certainly looked enough like the wild animal to have her heart racing.

"You're the sexy, well-endowed, straight-A honor student," he drawled, his voice low and sexy. Lani's breath caught again as Gregor prowled the dozen or so steps toward her. His chest glinted in the soft inner-ship lights, his muscles flexed as he slowly stalked her, much as any predatory animal would. "While I," he continued, ensnaring Lani both in his gaze and with his manner, "am the smart-aleck, brainy wannabe jock."

"You're not a wannabe jock," she said softly, reaching out a hand. Mere inches separated her fingers from his chest. Lani refused to slide forward the remaining few inches needed. "No wannabe jock could have a chest like that and arms and legs corded with muscles like you've got. You're one of those lucky few who fit in with the jocks as well as the brainy Honor list geeks."

Gregor smiled, and Lani watched him suddenly come to her all. She could easily feel the warmth of his skin radiating out to her, the heated press of male flesh and muscles. She let her legs part of their own volition, wanting to cradle him, embrace him in every way possible.

Gently, he turned her, so she crouched on the floor on all fours. Lani smothered a surprising bubble of giggles as they rose up. The floor was incredibly comfortable! It seemed to almost cocoon and give support to her hands and knees.

All thoughts fled as Gregor, hot and hard behind her, reached a hand down to finger her creaming pussy.

"You're so wet," he breathed into her ear. "Creaming so much, and all for me."

Lani couldn't help the shiver that ran through her body at his heavy words. They seemed almost thick, as if he couldn't quite get the words out through the emotion clogging his throat.

Lani could feel every inch of his skin, his warm fingers rubbing her outer labia, smearing her cream all around her swollen pussy. She moaned as his fingers skimmed tender nerves and ran lightly over her sensitive flesh.

"Gregor," she panted lightly, amazed at how with just a few strokes he could have her desperate for his possession. "Gregor, I need to feel you inside me."

"I know," he growled sounding like a man practically at the brink of his patience. He stroked her with longer, harder strokes, letting her feel how close to the edge he walked. "And knowing how much you want and need me turns me on like little else could. Can you feel how much I want you, Lani? What sort of reaction my body has to yours? How close you make me come to completely losing it?"

Lani gasped, and not only because Gregor had inserted three fingers into her swollen pussy. She realized with a blinding flash she *wanted* to make him lose control. Wanted to push him beyond his boundaries and make him explore his depths as much as he pushed her to do so.

With that knowledge came empowerment. Lani turned herself slightly and reached back so she could wrap two fingers in a tight circle around the thick root of his erection. She gently squeezed a little, enjoying the moan of approval Gregor gave her.

"Are you happy to trust me with a lot of control, Lani?" Gregor asked huskily. He had to clear his throat and then continued. "I think we could have a lot of fun together with this if you would."

Lani had known in some part of her it would come to this. She had known sooner or later, most likely sooner, there would come the time she needed to hand control and trust over to Gregor. Somewhere deep inside her, her intuition had known.

"Yes, I think I do, Gregor. Make love to me, please."

For a split second, a frown marred her face as Gregor's strong, warm, large hand put pressure on her neck, urging her to bend down.

"Keep your hand on my cock, use your other arm to cushion your face."

Lani could feel the warmth, the genuine caring behind his words. She smiled and obeyed him. This position raised her ass high in the air.

Lani felt slightly foolish for all of ten seconds. Until Gregor circled his fingers once more around her dripping pussy and, gathering some of the cream there, gently swirled her back passage.

The sensations, sensitive and tight, were amazing. She squirmed, just like the virgin she was there.

"Uhh…" Lani had no idea what to say, how to explain, particularly when the sensations bombarding her body and brain from his roaming fingers there were so pleasant she never wanted it to stop.

"Shh…" he soothed her, calming her sudden fear. "This will need time and preparation, I know. You did say you were a virgin here, didn't you, Lani?" Lani nodded her head, not wanting to say anything as she looked up and back at him from her position on the floor. The grin Gregor gave her spoke purely of a dominant male's excitement and happiness.

"Oh yeah, baby. This will definitely take special planning and timing. Unfortunately, it's not on the cards for today."

Lani heaved a sigh of relief as he moved his fingers away from her hidden passage. Wiping them on his thigh, he returned to her pussy. She tried a few times to fist his fully engorged cock, but with the delicious sensations at her ass, not to mention the fireworks going on around her damp slit, it was incredibly hard to keep her balance, let alone try to pleasure him as well.

"That's okay, baby," he crooned to her as he lifted her hand away from his straining cock. "I have a feeling this time is more about you than me. We'll come back to that another time."

Lani smiled and let her hands pillow her head. She felt sad, but grateful at the same time. She closed her eyes and concentrated on the amazing sensations her body was sending to her. She wanted to memorize this, think of it a million times when she was eighty and old and alone with her pets.

Gregor now stroked her with sure and steady fingers. Lani's whole world narrowed to her clit and pussy and to the sensations Gregor imposed on her. Within another half dozen caresses, she knew she stood on the verge of climax.

"Gregor," she moaned again, wriggling her ass and pushing back to feel the throbbing heat of his cock. Not wanting him to be left out completely, she moved her hand back for a short moment, let her fingers tighten around the base of his shaft. She gently tugged him, fisted him once and then moved her hand to his hips, urged him to come closer to her.

Surprisingly, he followed her brief lead, crouching over her. Slowly he lodged the tip of his massive erection in her pussy. She moaned and returned her hands back to pillow her head. The weight of his body lightly covering hers and pressing her into the soft floor seemed to be utterly erotic, and so dominant/submissive she felt her mouth water with the naughty sensations of being dominated.

"This won't last long, Lani," he taunted her, breathing heavily into her ear as he crouched his body fully over hers. He seemed somehow sinister and tender simultaneously. When he nibbled on the bottom of her ear, she moaned and tried to drive the tip of him far deeper inside her.

"Shit, you're tight, woman," he grunted as he pressed another inch deeper inside her. The angle he penetrated her was so deep and so tight, and just so damned good, she wanted to let herself explode from the simple act of him lodging himself inside her.

With another grunt, he pressed a bit more in.

"Please," she panted, knowing she wouldn't last much longer. "Just do it," she said breathlessly.

Gregor bit gently into the arch of her neck, and in one fierce thrust rammed into her to the hilt. If Lani had had any breath left, she would have screamed in delight. He seemed so incredibly thick she feared for a breathless second she would split. Yet he pulsed deeply inside her, stretching her like no one else ever had.

They sat like that a moment, and Lani let her body adjust to his thick meat throbbing inside her core.

"You are so thick, G," she panted, lifting herself up slightly. She wallowed in the comfort of Gregor's warm hand as he pressed her shoulder gently, indicating for her to return to her former position.

"Just wait, little girl," he purred as he withdrew his cock from her gloving pussy. "This is only the beginning."

Lani felt her heart flutter and her stomach turn over as he began to move in and out of her tight slit. She closed her eyes, to better feel every movement he created inside her, and she gasped as her heartbeat accelerated as he worked in and out of her body.

Just as she could feel herself begin the climb toward climax, Lani felt a thick, creamy finger press against her anal opening.

"Gregor!" she cried out, surprised and ecstatic at the sensations his thick finger invoked.

"Just because you aren't ready to take my cock back here, darling, doesn't mean I don't want this tiny opening stretched a little. Damn, you're tight. I can't remember the last time I had a virgin."

Pumping his cock the full length into her pussy, and now with one finger knuckle-deep in her ass, Lani felt as thoroughly possessed and reamed as she ever had in her entire life.

"More, Gregor," she pleaded, completely unashamed now. "I need more of you, right NOW!"

"My pleasure, Lani. It will be my pleasure."

Lani gasped in mingled pain and pleasure as Gregor bit gently down on her neck once again, obviously remembering how much it had affected her previously. Even so, he managed to hit a few sensitive erogenous zones with his delicate bite.

His thick, hot cock rammed in and out of her clasping pussy, making wet, slapping noises and causing shots of electrical sensations all over her body. The finger he had only barely up her ass stroked her sensitive inner walls, making her feel claimed and possessed as never before.

Everything built up inside her, until she didn't know what to do or think. All she could do was feel, feel his cock, his finger, and his mouth all over her body.

And in that one second, Lani exploded as surely as if a bomb had detonated inside her head and chest. She screamed, feeling her pussy *and* her ass contract, and her heart sped up until she feared she might pass out.

She had never experienced an anal orgasm before. It felt absolutely phenomenal. She dimly heard Gregor behind her groan into her neck as his thick cock jerked deeply inside her.

Shaking, all her muscles twitched in release. She didn't even have the energy to fight as Gregor gently spooned them and lay them back down on the warm floor.

Closing her eyes again, she tried to catalogue how her body had reacted to all its stimulation. She wanted to remember this moment in perfect clarity and detail forever.

As she took stock of her body and the zinging, twitching muscles, she felt a bit of disappointment as Gregor withdrew his cock, and a small amount of warm seed flowed down her thigh.

Gregor's solid, muscled arms wrapped around her shoulders and drew her to him and his body's heat. Spooned, they lay for a moment on the floor, as their breaths calmed down, her muscles stopped shaking, and their heartbeats returned to normal.

"Now that," Gregor said after a few moments, "was a brilliant way to start. I can't wait 'til we dock and I can really begin to show you some moves."

Lani laughed and snuggled closer into his chest. The climate-controlled room had begun to feel chilly against her naked skin, but the warmth of Gregor's body soon heated her again.

"If you have too many better moves than that, my head might really explode. That whole situation was absolutely fantastic."

"Just you wait, Lani," Gregor said smugly, helping her to stand up. "We'll both teach each other things we never realized."

Smiling and shaking her head, Lani followed Gregor to the back of the ship where they had stored their few spare suits and the tiny cleansing cubicle stood.

They both had minute-long steamshowers, mindful of the small amount of precious supplies they had. Climbing into her suit, Lani watched as Gregor also dried and clothed himself. Within a strangely short period of time, they were both back at the control panel, just as they had been not ten minutes before.

Feeling slightly unreal, Lani shifted on the seat. When her inner muscles twinged she smiled slightly to herself. It had certainly been real, and absolutely fantastic. She couldn't wait until they landed either, but for many different reasons.

Chapter Eleven

એ

Lani puffed as she pushed back more palm fronds. She and Gregor had been hiking for what seemed like hours. Hours and hours in fact, but the sun had barely moved, so in reality it couldn't have been too long.

Lani kept sending grateful prayers to the goddess that she had kept her fitness at a decent level. Otherwise she'd be almost tempted to whine like a baby about the steep incline they seemed to be taking an age to climb.

Yet every time she thought to complain, she recalled Leif. The unpalatable thought of her godson maybe being in trouble was more than enough to keep her going and not complaining. Finally, she decided to voice the one question that had been spinning in her mind since she had received Leif's message.

"Why would someone attack Leif and his parents' camp?" she asked. "I mean, it's not as if they were doing anything wrong. Marth was always most particular in her checking the scene first. She and Dany had this whole Expedition thing down pat by now. Any permits or approvals they would have needed she would have taken care of, and it's not like this place is in the middle of a land war, or an insurrection or anything."

Gregor shrugged and checked his compass once more. "Maybe they trod on someone's foot?"

Lani pushed more fronds out of her way as Gregor began leading again, but her mind still mulled over the questions.

"Even if they had, Dany was proficient in numerous languages. Between him and Marth they should have been able to explain or talk their way out of anything. Besides, at the faintest hint of problems, they would have packed Leif out of there. Even if they had stayed and tried to smooth over an issue, they would have made Leif leave."

"Well, we should know any minute now. According to the map they logged, we should be pretty much coming on top of where they had planned their base camp."

Lani took a few deep breaths, trying to prepare herself. She and Marth had gone through school together, and while they hadn't been as close after her Bonding with Dany, they had remained good friends. Lani had spent as much time as she could with them, and their friendship had remained stable. They both knew they could call on one another if ever the need arose.

Lani felt a wave of grief overcome her, but she swallowed hard and pushed it away. She needed to focus on Leif, needed to work out what happened and then when they all returned home she could indulge in her grief.

"Ah!" Gregor murmured. "Here we go!"

Lani smiled sadly as he led her through the last of the foliage and into a clearing. The campfire had been long since put out, and from the freshly settled dirt, Lani felt sure the Amazons had cleaned up what would probably have been signs of a major scuffle.

The Dany she had known would never have gone down without an almighty fight. Gregor stood watching, giving her space and room to breathe.

Lani walked around the tidy campsite, touching the familiar pans and pots, books and journals. Everything had been neatly packed up, and while Marth was an organized soul, Lani still had a feeling the Amazons must have helped put the entire campsite into order.

When she found Marth's diary, she was not surprised at the tears that prickled hotly in her eyes. Lani picked the small bound book up, holding it close. She would take this and give it to Leif when they met up.

Quickly placing it in her small bag, wanting to get over the worst of the pain as fast as possible, Lani walked a quick circuit of the campground. She could tell that the Amazons, or someone, had done a hasty cleanup. The only things that really stood out as being missing were the blankets Lani knew Marth always took with them.

Frowning, Lani turned to where Gregor still stood, on the edge of the clearing.

"Someone took the blankets," she said, her mind frozen and blank, unable to think coherently. Gregor didn't say anything, he merely pointed to where two fresh, raised mounds of dirt were on the very edges, near the trees and palms.

"I would bet the Amazons buried your two friends, most likely binding them tightly so they could be transported back home for a proper burial later."

Lani felt the now seemingly ever-present tears sting her eyes again. "Oh" was all she could manage to say as her throat choked up.

Blinking the tears back once again, determined not to cry like a baby, Lani crossed over to where the large mounds lay. Her legs were rather wobbly, so when she reached the edge of the simple grave, she sank to her knees, not wanting to embarrass herself by collapsing.

"Hey there," she said softly, not wanting Gregor to think her too much of a nut for speaking to a grave. "Wow, bet you didn't think this would be how we'd get together when you called to say goodbye before leaving."

Lani blinked away more tears, her voice growing even hoarser, until she practically whispered under her breath.

"I know Leif is a man now, of age and everything, but I swear I'll be there for him, take care of him, just like I promised all those years ago. So don't you worry, you don't need to hang around for him. You go off on your Explorings with Dany. Leif and I will be just fine. We'll muddle through it all. I promise."

Lani felt a heavy, warm hand press down on her shoulder. Despite the heat, she shivered, slightly chilled. She had always hated goodbyes. No matter how permanent or temporary they always made her teary, made her want to hold tighter and just cry.

"It'll be okay. We'll find the Amazons, get Leif, and they'll bring us back here and we can do whatever you and Leif decide on."

Lani nodded, and hiccupped, smiling through the couple of tears that had managed to escape. "I'm fine, I just hate saying goodbye. I'm so rotten at it."

Lani felt her heart melt a little as Gregor just smiled down at her, and carefully helped her to her feet.

"I don't think anyone is particularly adept at saying goodbye to a good mate. Don't worry about it."

Lani sighed and turned her attention to Gregor, slightly ashamed as her eyes began to water again. She blinked them away, this time for good as she saw the compassion and understanding shining in his dark gray eyes.

Gregor didn't say anything more, he just pulled her closer to his warm body. Hating herself, the situation, and the world at large, Lani buried her face in his shoulder and wept. All the fear and sadness she had been suppressing since the moment she had received the missive from Leif burst forth and she sobbed her heart out.

The minutes ticked by and Lani let her emotions slowly drain away. She sniffed, chuckled wetly and dug out the handkerchief she had purposely placed in her pocket of her skinsuit. Blowing her nose and avoiding Gregor's eyes, she looked everywhere around camp except at him. Surprisingly, he caught her under her chin and turned her face to look directly at him.

"There's no room for shyness in grief, Lani. No shame in letting it all go. You've been incredibly strong, and will need to continue to be so when we reach Leif. If you can't let it out here, then it will be far worse for you later."

Lani wrinkled her nose as if she smelled something bad.

"I know. I just hate crying. It seems like such a weakness, and it invariably makes men uncomfortable. I didn't mean to put you in that position."

Gregor shrugged, but kept his grip firm but not rough on her chin. "Do you see me acting awkward? Do I seem embarrassed to you? I've seen enough travesties in my life. An extremely short bout of well-deserved tears won't have me running for the hills."

Lani chuckled. "Okay. Point taken. I've got Marth's journal, which I'm sure Leif will want later. We can come back for their packs when we come back for...them, I suppose. Anything worth stealing will probably already be gone." Lani stepped reluctantly out of his warm embrace, smiling her gratitude to Gregor as he gently let her go. With fresh eyes, she scouted around the camp.

"How do we find the Amazons?"

Gregor turned to her, smiling engagingly. Lani's breath hitched. He looked so much younger with the faint orange-red glow of the main sun shining down on his handsome face, his mouth opened wide with the grin. He looked younger and so handsome Lani wanted to pull him down there and then, in the middle of a dangerous jungle and ride him until they both fainted from the sweaty exhaustion.

Or she did, until he opened his mouth to speak and broke the spell.

"Well, we could always get lost in the jungle and wait for them to *rescue* us."

Lani shook her head. "You know, Wonder Boy, you were really onto a great thing until you spoke and ruined it all. Your face, the sunset, your patience with embarrassing feminine tears, you were going brilliantly until you opened that stupid mouth of yours."

She laughed to herself as Gregor looked puzzled. "Ruined what? How? Huh?" Checking Marth's journal was safely tucked away in her bag, Lani snickered. "Don't worry about it, it's far too late now, the damage is done. How are we *really* going to find the Amazons? Do they have a permanent base?"

"I think so. Max, my business partner, gave me some coordinates and it's not a long distance from here. Hopefully they're still there. If not, I can comm Max for an update, and we can work from there."

Lani shrugged and waved her hands in front of them. "Then lead on, oh Illustrious Leader."

Gregor raised his eyebrow at her. "You're in a weird mood, aren't you?"

Lani shrugged again. "No more weird than at any other time. I'm just trying not to faint from exhaustion here. But we need to keep moving. I won't really be able to settle until I know Leif is okay, anyway."

Gregor grinned, a lecherous, thoroughly sexual grin. "Oh, he'll be perfectly all right. Completely exhausted and sexually satisfied beyond his wildest dreams, but in perfect health. Don't you worry about that."

Lani frowned at him as they moved back into the jungle. "You know, I'm almost beginning to believe you when you talk about these Amazons and their prowess."

Gregor threw her a grin over his shoulder. "Trust me, little girl, it's even better than what you think."

Lani grinned as she looked at the dense foliage they passed through. "If they really are like that, how the hell will I convince him to come home?"

Gregor chucked, a dark, utterly masculine chuckle. "If you really can't convince him, the Amazons will chuck him out and insist he go home with you. It might take him a few days to start talking to you again, but he'll get over it. Most of them do."

Lani bit her lip. She hadn't even *really* considered he truly might not want to be rescued. Leif was no longer a young boy, he had been a man legally for a few months now, and for close to a year maturity-wise.

Lani knew she certainly had no real right to "force" him to come back with her. What if he had fallen in love and not just lust with one of the women? Or what if he simply didn't want to come back with her to his home?

She knew Marth and Dany would expect her to at least *try* and convince him to either join the Guild or get him settled with a properly paying job, but essentially the man was his own person now. If he had changed his mind about entering the Guild, there really was nothing keeping him on their home planet.

Lani shook her head and decided not to borrow trouble. No sense in worrying about situations until she knew exactly what Leif would decide. She took a deep breath and decided to concentrate on the jungle instead. Not to mention the delectable ass walking directly in front of her.

As they passed through an even more dense section of the jungle, Lani felt herself almost hypnotized by the sexual sway of Gregor's hips and ass. Finding herself increasingly sexually uncomfortable, for it wasn't as if they could stop *now* to relieve some of her tension, Lani went back to her *other* train of thought.

She began to think about different bribes she could offer her young godson if there came the need.

Frowning, realizing she didn't have a whole lot to bribe him with, particularly when the bunch of Amazonian women could offer what most men just past their majority eighteenth wanted, complete and utter sexual satisfaction, Lani set her mind to busily thinking.

She would come up with something eventually, she hoped.

Chapter Twelve

ॐ

Leif pulled futilely on the soft leather restraints that had been clasped around his wrists seemingly hours ago. "Sarha," he panted as he strained up as much as his bound body could manage.

Never had he had such satisfaction, yet simultaneously have the burning desire for more and more. At times he wondered if Sarha were actually a drug he would never free himself of.

Her hair and eyes mesmerized him, her body and creamy, rich taste had become so ingrained into his skin and makeup he wanted more of her even when she allowed him to touch and taste her.

Leif now knew with a shattering certainty a man could go mad with lust. He felt a giddy sense of satisfaction to know he would never in his later life go mad. For if anything could drive a man to it, this was it, and he seemed to be passing the "test" very well.

Sarha lay cradled between his spread thighs, rolling his sac delicately inside the warmth of her mouth. This more than anything proved to him how much he had grown to love and trust this woman in such a short time span. With his future lying inside her heated mouth, he only experienced the eroticism of the moment, not a quiver of worry.

Indeed, Sarha had taught him much in the last— How long had he been here? Leif now knew and fully appreciated that a small amount of pain, carefully and placed with talent, could make him shoot his load faster than anything else he had ever known.

Leif wished like fury he could cup Sarha's much-beloved face, run his hands through the silky strands of her gorgeous hair. He acknowledged to himself, much as his father had told him before, that a few nights spent amongst the Amazonian women was as close to heaven as any man could rightfully lay claim to.

And for the first time, he had two women pampering him, not just his Sarha.

The second woman, Lita, he thought her name was, crouched facing backward on his chest. She had an incredibly long, brown ponytail, which tickled his chest as she moved. She bent down, alternately sucking his erect cock inside her mouth, and teasing him with biting nibbles across his waist and hips.

Yet her bending down to do this gave him a perfect view of her pink, pouting pussy and lips wet with her own dew. No matter how hard he strained and bucked, he simply could not reach his face down to that perfectly pouting pussy and anus.

After hours of them both caressing him, covering him with their gentle, teasing touches, Leif truly thought he would go mad. Lita finally raised herself from his cock and turned to face him.

"Kiss me," he whispered hoarsely, his voice being rusty from his ecstatic shouts, "Let me taste myself on you."

Smiling sweetly, she complied, and Leif wondered whether this was heaven or hell. Somehow, they seemed to merge together until he truly could not tell the difference. Greedily, desperately hungry like that of a starved man, he kissed Lita, ate at her mouth.

She tasted sweet and hot, wet like the most succulent of fruits. Leif thrust his tongue into her mouth, eager to lap up everything he could from her. Lita tangled her tongue with his, proving herself just as eager and hungry.

Fiercely, he tried to reap all he could of this moment. And then he felt it.

One thin, greasy-slick, feminine finger entered his anus. He shouted at the sensation, as if a million nerves had been touched and fired up. The sensation truly exploded though his system, ran straight through his head, chest and simply charged through his cock like a stampeding herd of *helphumps*.

He shouted, the incredible blend of pain and pleasure blending like nothing he had experienced before in his life. Even his many times and experiences with Sarha, and now Lita, had not prepared him for the experience of his anus being taken over by his beautiful Amazon Sarha.

Lita drank his cry, her delicate hands cupping his face, lifting it higher so she could nibble his lower lip.

"Do it again," she whispered softly against his lips. Leif didn't know if she talked to him or Sarha. "He loves it, don't you, baby? I want to feel that jolt of electricity run through you again."

Leif simply chuckled softly. He had loved it. It had hurt very slightly, yet the pleasure of the sensation, of the alien, foreign nerve endings being set alight by Sarha's tiny, delicate finger had brought him more ecstasy than he had ever believed possible.

He wanted it again almost as much as Lita obviously did—not that he thought he would ever admit it.

Sarha moaned in the back of her throat. Leif would recognize her voice, those little sounds of pleasure of hers anywhere in the galaxy. And then she started stroking his inner anal walls, pressing her small finger even deeper into his anal passage.

The pleasure seared through him. He would never have believed anyone had they explained the pleasure a man could feel through his anal passage. Yet here he lay, bound to a rickety cot-bed, being teased like a sexual slave of the best kind, having his ass tormented by the two most beautiful women in the entire galaxy.

He would never have believed it, and no one back home would ever believe the tales if he told them. The fact he would keep most of these memories as well-hidden secrets drove him even wilder.

Lita continued to kiss him, murmuring softly as she drank his cries of absolute pleasure. Sarha continued her explorations, every now and then she would hit a particularly sensitive spot he never knew even existed, and his hips would buck, thrusting his sac more deeply into her mouth, making her moan with the pleasure.

It almost seemed as if he were in a dream, or the hottest fantasy of his entire life. He had one woman sitting on top of him, kissing him fiercely and having her ass bounce enticingly against his iron-hard cock. He had another woman, a woman he had come to love and crave, suckling him and exploring his ass with one delicate finger.

He had never before experienced such intense pleasure, let alone believed it existed.

He could feel the lust rising in him, growing and growing like some fierce, wild beast. He knew he would be made to feel even more before he could come, yet even now he thought he would self-combust from the incredible joy singing through his body.

Lita drank from his mouth, eagerly sparring her tongue with his, he devoured her taste, as eager as she to feast upon her delicate, feminine flesh.

On and on the situation rose, coming closer and closer to the inevitable climax, yet the two women drew it out as if they had all the time in the world. As far as he was concerned they never needed to stop.

Both he and Lita waited in fascination as Sarha added a second slim finger into his anus. Lita seemed particularly enthralled with the sight, but Leif merely watched Sarha's face. She seemed to be concentrating, but he could tell from the flush across her face, neck and chest that she was incredibly turned on.

After days of studying the beautiful woman, Leif knew that her power, her sexual control over him turned her on impressively. Leif watched her as his body nearly burst from the pleasure she gave him.

He relaxed his sphincter muscles, hoping this would ease her presence as well as heighten his own pleasure. What he hadn't planned on was the second, longer feminine digit reaching an inner bud.

A very sensitive, masculine, well-hidden bud.

Pleasure ripped through him once again. His back arched and even though he thought he would cry out, so intense was the pleasure that nothing emerged from his mouth.

A soundless cry tore through him as his body seemed electrocuted from the pleasurable lust filling him.

"Oh yeah, baby," Lita crooned to him, cupping his head as his mouth silently screamed. She kissed his cheek as she sank slowly, inch-by-inch, down on his throbbing shaft.

"I swear you are the best ride I have had in years," she panted as she plunged and lifted over him. Even the gloving, wet heat of her pussy added to his torment and pleasure. Lita fulfilled one need, but only one woman, a sweet little blonde who currently suckled his balls and resided in his ass could completely answer his silent prayers.

Leif, even in his wildest, wickedest dreams and fantasies, had never envisioned something as unique as this. He thrust his hips upward, not wanting to relieve the pressure in his ass, but desperately seeking to move deeper into Lita's sweet pussy.

"Turn his ties," Lita gasped. Leif didn't understand what she meant, but he cried out at the loss of the warm, slim fingers and the wet heat that had been surrounding his balls.

He vaguely saw Sarha wipe her fingers on a cloth, then scurry to the head of the bed on which he and Lita lay, pounding away. With a flick of her wrists, he could feel the ties loosen enough that he could place his wrists together and have some leverage.

Barely thinking, he flipped Lita and himself over so he could drive even deeper into her. With her on her back, and him having this new leverage, he knew he could rush them to orgasm within a few moments.

He vaguely heard the faint *snap-click* of a tube being opened and then shut. Leif chose to ignore it, however, being solely focused on the beautiful woman beneath him. For a moment, he wished his hands were free, so he could palm her breasts, squeeze them together enticingly, yet the warmth surrounding his hard-to-bursting cock was more than enticing enough for the moment.

Next time, he promised himself, much as he had any number of times so far.

Small, warm hands gripped his ass and pulled his cheeks slightly apart. Gasping in shock, Leif paused mid-stroke and turned his head to look over his shoulder. Sarha knelt behind him on the bed, a short, thin dildo strapped across her luscious pussy. Leif's mouth opened in shock.

Would she really…?

He didn't even have time to finish his thought before the chilly, lubed head of the small dildo penetrated his ass.

He felt an incredible mixture of pain and pleasure, and though he would never admit it to anyone else in the entire galaxy, the thought of this woman he loved, this Amazon, penetrating his ass, turned him on more than he could ever have believed possible.

Lita had turned slightly beneath him, so she, too, could watch as Sarha penetrated him. Sarha pushed herself, holding his hips for the required leverage, until he could feel the faint scratchiness of her pubic hair against his ass cheeks.

"Pound into me, lover," Lita said huskily, pulling his hips toward her.

Slowly, his ass flaming with its fullness, Leif gently pulled his cock out of her gloving warmth until only his swollen, throbbing head lay notched in her opening.

This action caused him to move even farther back onto Sarha and her dildo. Sarha held herself steady, one arm on his shoulder, the other around his waist. She delicately nibbled on his shoulder, in just the spot he *knew* she knew was especially pleasurable for him.

The whole scene as it flashed through his head seemed so erotic, he could barely contain himself. When he plunged himself balls-deep back inside Lita, instead of feeling the dildo slip from him, he felt Sarha follow him down onto the bed.

The three of them squashed together, Leif braced himself on his knees, and simply moved his hips. This afforded his cock the friction of Lita's pussy, but his ass also could feel every thrust and move Sarha made in tandem with his own movements.

He wanted it to last forever. He wanted to etch this entire scene into his mind and across his heart until his dying day. He never wanted the pleasure, the heavy, fulfilling satisfaction of his ass being penetrated by this woman to go away.

He barely made it ten minutes.

The sensations erupting through his body were more than he had ever experienced in his life. His ass felt full, heavy, and his cock was being milked by an incredibly tight pussy, and Lita was squeezing down on him to give him even more pleasure.

He shouted, and his cock spurted so long, he wondered if he would ever become erect again. Jet after jet of his seed shot into Lita. He could feel the excess running down her thighs, and dripping on his own muscled thigh.

He collapsed next to Lita, panting and so out of breath as if he had been running for days. Sarha, still lodged deeply in his ass, curled behind him. The three of them lay for a few moments, panting, trying to regain some equilibrium.

Finally, Sarha wriggled and pulled herself from his ass.

"That was wonderful," she said softly. Leif turned slightly, as much as he could while still bound and looked at her. She smiled down at him, her love and passion shining brightly in her beautiful blue-green eyes. She blew him a kiss, and then looked over to where Lita lay, still panting.

"Wanna swap positions?" she asked her friend and tribemate cheekily.

Leif groaned and dropped his head back on his arms. He prayed, but for what, he wasn't sure. He loved every moment these women spent with him, never wanted it to stop. But they certainly gave new meaning to the word "Insatiable".

He moaned when Lita drew a deep breath and replied to Sarha, "Sure. But this time, I want to wear the strap-on."

Leif wriggled his fingers. He never would have guessed women like this existed. But he certainly didn't want to argue when he had no idea how long it would last. He mightn't be able to walk by the end of it, but he would be one very, *very* happy man.

Chapter Thirteen

෨

The man sat patiently in the middle of the jungle. He could wait. It wasn't as if he had anything else to do with his life.

He lifted his SearchGlasses to his eyes once again. His minion had already appraised him of his enemy's arrival, along with the woman he had labeled to be the "bait". And so he had made his way to the spot he had long ago decided to make his ambush point.

He knew from his minion's reports the direction his quarry would be coming from, and coupled with the knowledge his quarry was on his way right at this minute, he didn't need anything other than that.

After all, the quarry traveled with a woman. Women were a hindrance and generally useless. They whined constantly and they knew nothing about fighting or other manly pastimes. He just knew the bait would not interfere with his plans at all.

The man had complete confidence in himself and in his perfect plan. He would have his revenge. He had been making and plotting his plan for revenge for months. He had turned the plan over and over in his mind and looked at every possibility. He had thought it through and included variances for every contingency that could possibly arise.

When his messenger had been slain, he had planned for it. When the quarry had brought this particular woman with him, he had planned for it.

The man prided himself on his skill, on his plans. *Nothing* could go wrong.

He would succeed. His vengeance would be set in motion. Once he killed the quarry, the two *real* culprits, the man and the woman who had been present when his half-brother had been slain, would come after him for their own revenge.

Even this he had planned for. In fact, the beauty of his plan was the two culprits coming after him lay as the heart of his own plan.

Once the three people were dead, he could then rest. His half-brother and Uncle's souls could rest.

And everything would be balanced.

The man kept his SearchGlasses out. He checked the time against the orange-red main sun. The quarry and the woman should be coming soon. The man shifted slightly, perfectly happy to wait however long it took. He had been waiting for months, a few more minutes or hours here or there would make absolutely no difference.

Just then, he saw a rustling of the fronds. He double-checked through his SearchGlasses.

Perfectly on time, he mused to himself. As always, his plan ran utterly according to schedule.

Phase One, the killing of the stupid woman bait as well as the cocky quarry would now begin.

Chapter Fourteen

&

After almost an hour of walking through the densest parts of the jungle since leaving Marth and Dany's main camp, Lani had tried to think through any number of things. She constantly found herself coming back to fantasizing about Gregor, but she diligently tried to focus on anything else. Now was most certainly not the time for tearing her clothes off and having a heated jungle romp.

Yet the thought of sweaty, hot, crazy jungle sex simply would not vanish from her mind. She couldn't decide if she had become a nymphomaniac sex fiend sometime in the last twenty-four hours, or if the combination of watching Gregor's ass sway and the steamy heat of the jungle were scrambling her usually quite logical mind.

In between heated fantasies of sucking Gregor off, not to mention numerous other delicious fantasies she diligently tried to ignore, she had at least been able to think of a million different things to try and tempt Leif back with. She didn't feel too confident in any of them, but she had also come to realize that Leif wasn't the silly kid he had been six months ago.

Deep inside, she had a surprising amount of faith in her godson, and had the oddest feeling he truly would, while maybe not admit it, see the logic in returning with her and continue on with his lifelong dreams of joining the Guild. Lani wrinkled her nose as she pushed yet another frond away from her face. She was almost certainly worrying for nothing.

Among other things, she had also found the most bizarre fascination staring and analyzing Gregor's footprints in the soft soil. When Lani found herself doing so, she shook her head and tried to concentrate on something else. She wondered if jungle fever started out like this.

And finally she had been left with analyzing the jungle itself surrounding them. She had seen any number of different butterflies, snakes and other assorted crawling creatures. Not wanting to freak herself out, she had decided to concentrate on the flora, instead of the fauna.

Twenty minutes later she could almost swear she could tell the differences between the greens.

The undersides of the fronds were one shade of green, the tops another. The vines creeping around the stems were a different shade of green again.

Immersed in so many varying shades of the one color, Lani found it amusing she could be so interested in the variance between them all. Tired of feeling hypnotized by the bunched muscles underneath Gregor's skin-shirt, not to mention the delectable view of his tight and oh-so-slightly swaying ass, Lani had found herself staring anywhere *but* directly in front of herself.

She would also bet a large number of credits Gregor, as well, was practically ignoring her, or the distraction she caused him, as the man had barely given her more than a few grunts to the couple of questions she had posed to him earlier in their hike.

She did, however, feel more than a small amount of pride in the fact that instead of slicing through all the wonderful vegetation they were hiking past, he, like her, simply pushed it out of their way. She was also incredibly grateful that he wasn't treating her like some simpering girl but like the partner she was.

Which meant she spent more than enough of her time also pushing large leafy plants out of her way.

She concentrated so heavily on the different greens, it came as a start to catch a glimpse of a completely unknown shade of green. A shade mixed with browns. Pure instinct had her stopping in her tracks and reaching the short distance forward to grab Gregor's shoulder and point out the new, utterly unknown color out to him.

Ironically, she had intended only to ask him if it were some foreign breed of snake she should be wary of, or any other hunting animal that might try to bite and kill her. Yet the bloodcurdling scream that came from the animal had her nearly shrieking like the most loathed form of girly-girl in fear.

A flash of light reflected from something practically in her face, and Lani instinctively closed her eyes. She heard Gregor grunt, and then she heard the unmistakable sound of him removing his beamer from his belt.

Relief happened to be the first emotion she felt, relief she had been able to stop Gregor walking into whatever the animal was. And knowing Gregor, if he had removed his beamer rifle, it had to be a pretty dangerous, deadly animal.

Pain overcame her relief quickly as she was thrown unceremoniously onto the ground. Lani tasted the dirt as her head was practically planted straight into it.

Coughing and spluttering, she managed to turn her head sideways and open her mouth to spit the dirt out. For a split second, she tallied her injuries. She had grazed her hands and legs on the assorted rocks, twigs and other debris littering the jungle floor, scraping small abrasions into her hands and wrists. They burned something fierce, but otherwise, she seemed perfectly unharmed.

Lani sat up onto her knees, gingerly looking around the heavy foliage of leaves and trees, wanting to see what kind of incredible creature could have shaken Gregor so much he felt in necessary to bodily throw her into the ground and fight it alone. Instead, she saw the back of Gregor as he dashed through a few of the fronds and started an incredibly noisy fight.

Lani sat back and took a deep breath, intending to yell at Gregor for being such a stupidly macho man. It wasn't as if she hadn't come across some oddly exotic and poisonous animals, as if she were some innocent, virginal young miss who needed the big, strong he-man to take care of her!

And then she heard the sounds of beamer rifles shooting.

Snakes and other assorted animals can't shoot beamer rifles, Lani numbly told herself. *Amazons don't wield them either,* her mind snidely injected. *Amazons still mainly rely on Old-World weapons unless they are fighting a war. Spears, slings and the such. And there's no way Gregor or his friend wouldn't have found out whether or not the Amazons were in a war.*

Lani stood up, brushed the dirt from her suit without even realizing what she did. Her stomach churned slightly as her worry grew. The only reason Gregor would be starting a beamer fight would be if an enemy had found them both here. Had she led him into a trap of some form?

Wincing slightly at the pain in her legs, Lani pulled out her own beamer and headed in the direction Gregor had taken. Surprise and disgust with herself overcame every other emotion. Since when had she been so slow to cotton on to anything? She must be losing her touch!

The murky green-brown wasn't an animal, or even a plant. As she crashed through less than a few feet of vegetation, she found it was a man she had never seen before, wearing an ancient army-style camouflage suit.

The man had what appeared to be a rather large beamer rifle which he swung with a heavy and possibly deadly force as Gregor tried to wrestle it from him. The deadly malice and sheer strength behind the much-larger man meant Gregor couldn't simply tackle the man to the ground. If his opponent managed even one solid hit, Gregor would be almost certainly knocked unconscious, and so he had to bide his time.

She couldn't see Gregor's own weapon, so he must had dropped it somewhere on the ground during the struggle. It must also be why he kept on letting himself get so close to his enemy, trying to disarm him. Lani shook her head, men and their stupid macho games! Why the hell hadn't he called out for her help?

Lani turned her rifle to stun and tried to get an unencumbered aim at the unknown man. With the large, heavyset man who appeared to have dark, lanky hair grappling so closely with Gregor, a clear shot seemed virtually impossible.

Gregor fought fiercely, but for once, maybe due to the unexpectedness of the fight as well as the extra forty or fifty pounds of sheer flesh and muscle his opponent had on him, her lover seemed to be losing ground in the fight. She winced as the heavyset man brought his beamer crashing down on Gregor's hand. Gregor cursed vocally, but actually managed to get a firm hold on the other man's beamer as well as his wrist.

As the two men grunted and wrestled with each other, Lani tried to let Gregor catch sight of her so he could keep their opponent still for a moment. Much as she simply wanted to rush in and start wresting as well, she knew she could be no help in the physical tussle. She needed to get a clear shot of the man so she could stun him. Lani made herself breathe deeply to quell the urge she felt so strongly to go into the fray and help her lover.

After such a long, exhausting journey where they had literally been on the go for nearly two days straight now, Lani fearfully questioned whether Gregor had the stamina to try and hold off the much heavier man for much longer.

The other man seemed bigger, stronger, more able to win the wrestling fight they found themselves locked in.

Her patience at an end, she called out.

"Dammit, G, give me a break here!"

Her lover grunted, and getting the man in a chokehold, turned them both around. Finally given a decent shot, Lani stunned the man, watching with satisfaction as Gregor released his hold and the man fell to the floor, an absolute dead weight.

Gregor spared her a smile, and then knelt beside the fallen man to check his vital signs. Lani stepped forward, pocketing her beamer after replacing the safety.

"Get me some sturdy vine to tie him up with, Lani."

Lani shrugged, a bit disappointed Gregor couldn't even think so thank her for her help. However, one quick look at his dark countenance and the wheels obviously turning inside his head, she had a feeling there was more than just a small bit of history behind the unconscious man and her lover.

Being careful not to snag and thus snap and break the vine, she unwound a number of feet's worth of the native green, creeping ropelike substance. Ignoring its slight stickiness, she wound it carefully into a neat bunch and headed back to Gregor.

When she handed it to him, he looked up at her and smiled.

"Thanks. I'm sorry you got dragged into this."

Lani's patience began to wane.

"You're sorry that *I* got dragged into this? Excuse me? Just who dragged whom? I seem to recall sending you that coding and requesting you to come with me."

Thoroughly out of sorts now, Lani pushed Gregor out of the way and bent down next to the unconscious man.

Quickly, though careful of his circulation, she bound the unknown man's hands together. The vine, although thin, seemed incredibly sturdy, and even the slightly sticky goop around it seemed to solidify into a nice paste to keep the man well restrained.

"You going to tell me about any of this? Or are you going to continue to play macho he-man and keep me in the dark here? Remember, you would have walked straight into it, and him, if I hadn't have seen something and stopped to question you."

Lani shut her mouth and tried to repress the simmering annoyance inside her. She had no idea when she had suddenly become shrewish, but she cringed at how awful she sounded.

In silence, she continued with her work, trying to calm her anger.

After tightly binding his hands, she pulled the vine down his body and began to repeat her actions with his feet. Gregor, thankfully, seemed to be keeping his distance from her, maybe for once he couldn't help but miss the heavy feminine annoyance that must have been positively radiating from her.

Or maybe he was thinking of what he was prepared to tell her about whatever the situation they found themselves in.

Lani bit her lip softly so she didn't mutter mean, incoherent sentences about the general stupidity of men as a gender of overprotective idiots.

Lani finished tying the most intricate triple-tight knot she could do and sat back to survey her handiwork. Swearing, she carefully looked over her bindings to make sure they were firm and secure. Unless the man had incredible superpowers, he wouldn't be breaking loose any time soon, particularly not half on his stomach with his face in the dirt and his arms and legs in a tightly controlled manner behind him.

Taking a deep breath, trying desperately hard to calm herself down, Lani turned and stood up. Gregor had, himself, stood and now leaned negligently against a tree, his arms and legs crossed in the picture of a man attempting to act casual.

He stayed silent, seeming to look to her to start the conversation.

Lani no longer wanted to tear into him, but was more interested in getting some answers. Calmly, with an even voice, she asked what she felt to be the most important question.

"Who is he, do you know?" Lani smiled cynically to herself. Why not start with the simple stuff? It seemed so much more rational than playing with the outraged female act.

156

Gregor looked down to the bound, unconscious man at their feet. He nodded and sneered, some unknown emotion flickering in his eyes. Lani watched, amazed, as a dam seemed to break forth from Gregor.

"I do believe you have just met Im'an Remington, one of the most wanted men by the Force. Max and his Bondmate, Kyli, ran into his half-brother, Am'ah, a few months ago. He was killed during the uprising between the Old Regime and the Rebels. Im'an was nowhere to be found, and their uncle died soon after that. Im'an obviously came back from whatever rock he had been hiding under to find the last of his family dead. Max and I had heard vague rumors that he had sworn vengeance on Max, Kyli and me."

Lani tried to order everything in her mind. "So he was following you—" she paused as Gregor shook his head impatiently.

"I seriously doubt it. Remington has always been a plotter, a planner, not a chaser. I just can't see the connection between your friends and me."

Lani closed her eyes. She knew Gregor hadn't meant to imply her friends were involved with a criminal, but the slight thrust hurt nevertheless.

Angry as she had been at Gregor, she could feel a huge well of annoyance build up inside her, aimed directly at herself. The possible ramifications clicked into place in her mind.

She opened her eyes again to stare blankly at the still unconscious man bound and tied on the ground. "He used Marth and Dany as bait," she stated quietly, still hoping it was all a big misunderstanding. The thought that two wonderful people, good friends of hers, could have been an unknowing part of some elaborate, utterly twisted plot hurt her more than their deaths themselves had.

Gazing at Im'an, she didn't see Gregor frowning and rub a hand over his face.

"Me," she whispered as even more of his plot seemed to light up in her mind. "He knew Leif, or someone, would be able to get a message to me. He probably knew I worked with you…"

"No," Gregor said huskily, taking her attention away for a split second. "He would only know that a kidnapped man, Leif or anyone else, would be enough for either myself or Max to come out here to find him. He would have used us that way. He might have known *of* you, but he always underestimated women."

Lani chewed her bottom lip as she thought.

The man beside them moaned a deep, pain-filled moan.

Gregor smiled nastily. "I bet he won't ever underestimate women again."

Lani cocked her head and looked at the trussed-up man who lay in the dirt. "I don't think he will underestimate women anytime soon either."

Gregor knelt down beside Im'an, who tried to turn, only to jerk as he found himself trussed up very sturdily. When he opened his eyes, he saw Lani.

"Bait!" he sneered. Lani worried for a minute he would magically untangle himself, but instead, he simply seemed to grow smaller.

"A woman?" he gasped, "I could not possibly have been felled by a woman!"

"Deal with it," Gregor laughed, turning the man's attention solidly to him. "If you're very nice and answer my questions, we won't throw you to the Amazons to eat for dinner."

Lani felt pity for the man as he turned hate-filled eyes to Gregor.

"You! You were so arrogant, so cocky! You were the perfect quarry."

Gregor shrugged. "So what if I was? I at least had backup, anyone you had was too long gone to be any use in helping you. You should have trusted a woman to watch your back long ago. Maybe then you wouldn't be where you are. Now, about that little manner of gunrunning, slave smuggling, insurgence defying..."

The man began to spit out a number of curses. Gregor just smiled even more.

"I bet you can't wait to get back on Force soil. You'll be nothing but dust by the time your cell time is over."

Even though Im'an continued to heap curses upon both her and Gregor's head, Lani could see the fear and anger in his eyes. Whatever sins could be laid at this man's door, she knew with an instinctive certainty he would have return to him threefold. Lani smiled slightly to herself. Maybe a bit of Amazonian justice wouldn't go astray, if they could ever find their campsite.

Lani heard a strange bird-call. She cocked her head, having never heard it before and wondered what kind of bird would be hanging around after all the noise and scuffling they had been making.

Gregor, however, looked pleased. He returned a similar bird-call, whistling and clicking with his tongue.

"But maybe, just maybe, a bit of Jungle Justice, my very dear friend?"

"I am no friend of you, you murdering, cock-sucking—"

"Ah." Gregor casually stood up and brushed the dirt from his skinsuit. "With that dirty mouth and horrendous attitude, not to mention your underestimation of women, I'm thinking that you are about to have the pleasure of meeting your new captors."

Lani frowned, but understood as she saw a half-dozen extremely tall women walking through the brush. All of them approximately six-foot tall and buxomly statuesque, clad in differing leathers and belts, the women seemed imposing but somehow sensual at the same time.

Lani stood, understanding dawning that these were the women who had been taking care of Leif for the past few days. She owed them a debt she could never really repay.

She smiled at the youngest-looking one, a blonde with interesting blue-green eyes. The Amazon smiled widely back, seeming to be genuinely pleased to meet her. Lani noticed Gregor had sidled up to two of the older-looking women, and was gesturing to Im'an, while deeply in conversation with them. The young blonde came forward toward her.

"I am Sarha," she introduced herself. "You are Leif's Aunt Lani?"

"Yes," she said, truly pleased to meet the young girl. Honestly, she couldn't be more than nineteen or twenty. "You've been taking care of Leif?"

The young girl grinned, a knowing, sensual grin. "Yes, it has been my pleasure to take care of Leif. He is a wonderful man."

Lani laughed and hugged the woman, many of her fears and worries melting away. Just as she had hoped, Leif had almost certainly been having the time of his life. The fact this friendly, pretty young woman had been "taking care" of him made all of Lani's doubts and worries seem utterly unnecessary.

"Thank you so much, Sarha. I truly appreciate every single thing you have done for that young man. I hope he has behaved himself."

Another woman came up behind them, a sensual brunette a few years older than Sarha, but still much younger than Lani.

"He has behaved wonderfully. Many of us have helped…watch over him. He has, I believe, enjoyed himself immensely."

Lani shook her head. "I hope he will want to leave with me," she trailed off, not wanting to offend the Amazons. Both these two women seemed like part of a happy, friendly bunch, all of them appearing sensual and strong and simply amazing.

The older-looking woman, who seemed to be the one in charge of the group, turned to her.

"It is time for him to leave with you. He will leave when you arrive back with us. We will take this man with us, and when he has learned the first of his lessons, we will hand him over to the authorities."

As a group they all turned to look at Remington, and the man shivered. Lani refused to feel sorry for him. Amazons never hurt their "captives" more than they wanted. Maybe having the women in charge of him for a short time would do him a world of good.

As long as he ended up in the Force's hands, Lani didn't think she'd mind him getting a taste of his own medicine. She watched critically as two of the Amazonian women helped him to his feet.

They were by no means gentle with him, and yet they treated him with a certain respect. As if they realized how canny he was, and knew he would give them trouble if they allowed it.

It seemed to be the right mixture of femininity and dominatrix to work for him. He watched them all warily, as if sizing them up. Lani had a strong feeling that, unlike Leif, only the older, more savvy women would be "taking care" of this particular man.

Undoubtedly they would bring him down a peg or two, give him a number of hard, thoroughly enjoyable rides, and then hand him over to the Force. Lani smiled, jungle justice might be the best brand of "punishment" for this man.

Two of the women cut his foot bindings, holding his still bound arms carefully between them. They set the pace as the group walked to the Amazon's camp. Lani grinned wryly, as the journey took less than fifteen minutes.

She shot an amused-but-angry glance at Gregor. "You could have told me we were so close," she chided.

He grinned at her and shrugged. Lani couldn't reply, as she heard Leif's startled, "Aunt Lani. You're here…promptly."

Lani chuckled and ran out to meet him halfway. They embraced warmly, and Lani pulled her godson particularly tightly to her. She chuckled when he began to squirm in slight embarrassment, as men across the galaxy were wont to do. She linked her arm through his, but let him pull away slightly.

"You've been having fun, brat?" she asked cheerily.

He grinned cheekily at her, casting a hot glance to Sarha. "Oh yeah. I've had a wonderful time."

Gregor came over to them, glancing from Leif back to her.

"We can stay here overnight, and head out at first light tomorrow."

Lani noticed for the first time since the fight that Gregor wasn't really looking at her. A part of her deflated. She had known they were just an affair, a fling, but she had hoped it would last longer than two days.

Gregor continued, looking at Leif and around the campsite. "This time tomorrow, young man, you can be back at your lodgings. The Amazons and I will arrange for your parents' bodies and belongings to be shipped back safely. You can start the arrangements when you reach port."

Leif nodded solemnly. Gregor turned to leave without even glancing at Lani.

Lani frowned, debated whether she should chase after him and hit him, or yell at him and insist on a few answers to what the hell he thought he was doing.

And then she mentally saw the shrewish character she would seem to be if she did such a thing. She looked to Leif, who still had his arms around her, but was casting a longing glance at the beautiful Sarha.

Lani mentally sighed. Seemed like she wouldn't be the only lovelorn person on the ride back home. Even as she could feel a large chunk of her heart turn chill, shrivel and die, she hugged Leif even more tightly to herself.

She had things other than her soon-to-be-infamous two-day fling to worry about. Most likely one of them would be counseling her now-a-man godson on how to act like a man when ending a love affair, and maybe still retain a few pieces of his heart.

Taking a deep breath, Lani forced each and every thought of Gregor out of her mind. Leif most certainly needed to be the center of her attention right now. She was a mature woman, she could deal with her own heartbreak later. Turning Leif's face toward hers, she kissed his cheek warmly.

"Why don't you introduce me to some of your...friends," she teased him like she always had, even though try as she might to ignore it, a large part of her wanted to curl up into a small ball and cry.

Leif, not even really noticing her sadness, took her hand and walked her to one side of the camp where a small group of pretty young girls sat around and talked.

Lani smiled and tried to act normal—whatever the hell that now was.

Chapter Fifteen
Two weeks later

ɛɔ

Lani came to work with slightly red, still puffy eyes. She glared at her cubicle-mate, who tried to ask her if she was all right.

Idiot bastard Jym, she couldn't help but think. *Do I look all right?*

Lani sighed and chided herself. It wasn't as if poor Jym had a clue what was going on in her mind. Feeling repentant, she smiled at him weakly.

"Sure," she said huskily, her throat being raw from all the crying she had done during the night. "I just had a big night. I'm fine."

Jym nodded and congratulated her for the success of her new code. She smiled weakly, trying to look as excited as she should feel. She thanked him again and waited for him to leave. He had cast a worried glance over her, and then thankfully let her be.

Early the previous evening, she had received a comm from Jayd, one of her Supervisors. Apparently, while she and Gregor had been off-world, Management had been presented with her new code, and had been deeply intrigued.

Jayd had let them play with it, had taunted them to attempt to break it. Over twenty-four hours later, when none of the self-professed genius code-breakers had been able to do anything with it, when they were screaming at her in frustration from not being able to break the code, Jayd had smiled prettily at them and offered to show them how to break it.

She had then told them about Lani and explained about her plans and desires for the code. When Jayd had excitedly commed her the previous evening to explain her success, Lani had barely been able to fake a smile, let alone get excited about it.

Yes, she *was* ecstatic about her success, but with so much else weighing so heavily on her mind, she just couldn't rouse any joy. Lani knew her code would earn her prestige within Management, would go a long way toward advancing her career, yet not even that thought could get her out of the doldrums she currently resided in.

Even worse had been later in the evening, when she had gone to collect her mail. Lani really didn't want to think any more about what had set her off on a depressingly long crying binge the night before. She sat in her seat and gazed morosely at her holo-screen as it began to turn itself on.

It had been over two whole weeks since she, Leif and Gregor had left Xylone for home. Two weeks of working ridiculously long hours in the vain hope of wearing herself out so she couldn't dream when she fell asleep.

Not that anything she did worked.

She had been working herself into physical exhaustion at the gym. She had tried eating herself sick. She had used the most potent sleeping patches she dared, as well as hypnotizing herself to sleep. Not even working a fourteen-hour day helped to stop the dreams.

And then yesterday after the funeral, and she had received the letter from Marth.

Dearest Lani,

I rewrite this letter every six months or so, and once again I hope you never see this one. Hasn't my little Leif grown? I feel certain he has become sexually active, not that he has told me so, but I can't help worrying over him.

I know you will watch over him, look out for him. Let him make his own mistakes, but always be there to help pick up the pieces, much like Dany and I try to do.

Even so, I am finding, the older my little boy gets, the more it is YOU I worry about leaving behind. For my "little boy" is a man past his majority, and is no longer truly little – he will be off Adventuring and entering the Guild any month now, and it will be you who is left alone, and not Leif.

Don't be afraid to love, my friend.

No, I do not mean those sexual escapades you embark on with monotonous regularity. I mean to love, and to open your heart and let someone deep inside you. You know the ancient cliché…to fall in love as often as you can…to love not wisely, but too well…you studied the ancient poems just as I did.

For it's not so often we come across love, real, Bond-worthy love. And I fear if you find it and then hit a problem, or snag, you won't fight for it. You will fight every other war man or woman has seen, yet you will not fight for yourself.

So my most beloved friend, fight for love. I have the strongest feeling it'll be knocking you over anytime now.

Your friend,

Marth

Reading it, Lani had burst into tears, the floodgates ˌopening again. She had cried and cried and no matter how many times she had washed her face and sipped her vitawater, she had fallen back into her tears.

All that night she had cried, and only in the early morning hours had she begun to plan. She would confront Gregor, rage and expose her wounded heart if need be. She would win him back or be absolutely humiliated in the process.

But first, her mind insisted as nerves reared their ugly head, *I will check my mail like the coward I always seem to be of late.*

Lani opened her holo-screen, and a familiar fox pranced onto the screen. It was not the womanly vixen she had created, but a masculine fox, with a large chest and a cheeky sparkle in his silver-gray eyes.

I'm hallucinating, her tired mind insisted. A *sleep-deprived, tear dehydration-induced hallucination.*

But no, this did not seem to be a hallucination. The fox tempted her, snarling sexily at her in a deeply masculine voice she recognized from all of those dreams. "Decode me if you dare!" he said.

It was almost identical to her much earlier, half-forgotten original dare.

She opened the attachment, and there, in her own simplistic and feminine code she had sent to Gregor all those weeks ago, Gregor had now sent her a missive.

Barely letting herself breathe, she decoded the message, watching as it flashed upon her holo-screen.

Lani,

If you have missed me even half as much as I have missed you, meet me in the back of my cubicle.

Lani stared at the message, not quite able to believe it to be true. She thought back to her tears of grief over Marth and Dany. Thought back to her determination to try and win back Gregor.

For a moment she toyed with the idea of ignoring him as he had ignored her among the tribe of Amazon women. Yet he hadn't ignored her as such, merely pulled away, let her walk her own path.

She stood, and as if in a daze, walked over to Gregor's cubicle. A thousand thoughts of words to say, ways to seduce him, crossed her mind. She had been planning to seduce him today anyway. Why would his contacting her make this any different?

Early as the hour was, his lights hadn't been turned on. Maybe he wasn't in yet? Her naughty smile came back, seeming almost rusty after all the tears she had cried the night before. If he wasn't in yet, maybe *she* could lie in wait for *him*?

Even with a zillion naughty and utterly un-doable thoughts racing through her mind, she stepped into the cubicle, only to find her wrist grabbed, and her entire body pulled forward to a hot, well-known, masculine body.

Trying to swallow her moan of need and regret for so many days wasted, Lani wrapped her arms tightly around the solid, never-forgotten shoulders and neck of the man she had come to love.

She couldn't even get a word out to him. She could only feel his lips pressing insistently down on hers as his strong arms wrapped tightly around her waist and chest. She felt herself being dragged closely into him, crushed against his body.

She kissed him deeply, hungrily, uncaring she could barely breathe so tightly did he hold her. She didn't care what had changed his mind or what had been going on between them in the last two weeks. She only cared about tasting him now, smelling his unique scent and holding him close. She dug her short nails into him slightly.

He moaned, and she bit his lower lip gently. She wanted to chastise him, prove she wasn't some weak-willed woman who crumbled when he turned aside from her.

Gregor moaned again, and Lani could feel her panties get damp. She gasped. She was creaming and they had only kissed!

She felt Gregor gently push her away from him as they both panted for a moment in the darkness of his cubicle. Then Gregor changed their positions, and turned her so she faced the wall.

She smiled against the scratchy surface, feeling like some heroine from a cheesy vid, about to get cavity- or strip-searched by the big, bad Force member. And then she realized Gregor stood closer to the entrance of his cubicle and her body would be shielded by his much-larger one to anyone who happened to take a glance inside.

He pressed her into the wall of the cubicle, rubbed his hard erection between her ass and her back.

"I'm hard as steel for you, Lani. I've been waiting, wanting to give you time to grieve, but I just can't wait any longer. It's been two weeks, and I have to touch you, to taste you..." he trailed off and Lani could barely believe what she was hearing. *He'd* been waiting for *her*?

"But you ignored me on the ship!" she protested, breathless with the solid promise, the heat of his shaft rubbing her ass. She tried desperately to think. Had she ever told him of her fantasies of anal sex? She couldn't remember!

Sure, he had sexily inserted only one finger into her ass on the ship and in the shower, but that barely even scratched the surface of her fantasies. She didn't think she had been coherent enough to mention the true depths of her fantasies to him that day. And there simply hadn't been enough time at any other stage to go into depth and details with him.

Lani shivered, wondered for a moment if Gregor truly could read a woman's mind, as some of the more common gossip around the workplace said.

Gregor growled warningly, nipping her neck lightly exactly where she loved it so much that she turned to jelly.

"You had an eighteen year old, upset over his parents' deaths and deeply in love with an Amazon he had to leave. He needed his aunt to talk to and help calm him down. You didn't need me jumping your bones one minute and ogling you the next."

"Oh," she said softly.

"And who was ignoring whose calls all last week?"

"Ah," she gulped. "I unplugged my comm," she admitted, flashing her bare wrist at him, proving she wasn't wearing it.

"For that," Gregor breathed across her neck as he rubbed his shaft even harder into her ass, "I think I get some playtime tonight."

Lani moaned softly, wanting to sink into the floor, strip right here where anyone could walk in on them at any given moment, and spread her cheeks wide.

"What did you have in mind?" she uttered hoarsely, so turned on she could barely breathe.

"Well," he said through gritted teeth, "how do you feel about another bout of anal sex?"

Lani smiled and gulped at the same time. She felt vaguely relieved he couldn't see her face as she wasn't sure if she would look more nervous or ecstatic.

"I've always fantasized, but I hear it hurts like a son of a bitch."

Gregor chuckled softly, and Lani felt her knees weaken even more. If she got any more turned on she would likely collapse.

"Oh yeah, darling, it hurts, but it hurts so good you won't be able to bear it. You'll want to scream and cry and once I'm done prepping you, you will most definitely be begging for more."

Lani whimpered as he whispered these hot words in her ear, grinding his hot shaft against her the whole time. She wanted him inside her like she had never wanted anything before.

"Bond with me, Lani," he asked huskily. Lani blinked, certain she had imagined his last sentence.

"What?"

"Bond with me. These last two weeks have been hell. I've done nothing but fantasize about you and jerk myself off. I haven't even managed to look at another woman. No one else has appeal anymore."

Lani frowned, tried to turn around, but couldn't, he held her tightly, a willing prisoner against his wall.

"That's rather permanent, don't you think? Bonding isn't exactly something you can undo."

Gregor nipped at her neck, making her shiver and her blood pump even faster.

"I know what I want. You can take all the time you want to think about it. But I'll warn you right now, I'll spend every possible moment trying to convince you to Bond with me."

Lani remembered Marth's words to her, but she didn't want to make such an irreversible decision lightly.

"My place," he whispered naughtily to her, his hot breath caressing her ear, "the instant the shift finishes. Be prepared for a siege, Lani. I'm going to ream your ass, and you will love it and be begging for more of my cock and for more of me. By the time I'm even halfway done with you, you will be begging to Bond with me, and you'll be depressed that Bonding only lasts for eternity, and not beyond."

Slowly, inch-by-inch, he stood back. Lani gulped to realize she instantly lamented the loss of his body heat. Even as she whimpered with the need to call him back, she knew she needed room to breathe, needed to think and not have these giddy feelings.

Needed to squash the childish, shrieking need inside herself to just give in and say "Yes!" She wanted to Bond with him forever.

"Your place," she managed to say breathlessly as she tried to control the feelings deep inside herself. She nodded as she turned around. "Straight after the end of shift."

"I'll be heading home now," he said. "I've taken the day off. I want to...prepare."

Lani gulped as all sorts of wicked images crossed her mind. "I'll see you then," she whispered softly, brushing past him to leave.

She looked at the clock up high on the wall.

Six hours until the end of shift. Six hours until Gregor. Six hours until he would prepare and then ream her ass. On top of that, she had six hours to debate the wisdom of Bonding herself for eternity with the one man who could set her heart alight, who could make her knees go weak as jelly and who could undoubtedly bring every one of her fantasies to life.

Lani knew deep in her soul that Gregor was the man for her. He was the only man who could recognize and understand the darkness inside her, could even match that with his own darkness and desires.

They were as close to a matched set as seemed possible to be. If they were any more in tandem with their sexual desires they'd be damn twins. She checked the clock, dismayed to see only a minute had passed.

Five hours and fifty-nine minutes.

How the hell was she supposed to concentrate now?

Chapter Sixteen

Lani couldn't remember most of her day. She had been in a daze since leaving Gregor's cubicle. She couldn't concentrate, and to be honest, hadn't even been able to focus on the road as she negotiated the way to his lodgings. She thought she might have passed through some red signals, but again, she hadn't been focusing.

She grimaced as she realized she might be in trouble the following day at work, and not just for the run signals either. She hadn't managed to get a single line of coding done, let alone any of the numerous reports floating around on her desk.

Heated thoughts twisted through her mind. She remembered with startling clarity the feeling of Gregor pushing his thick fingers up her ass. She squirmed in her seat as she replaced that memory with the fantasy she had been having every damn single evening.

Of Gregor replacing those fingers with his thick, hot cock. Gregor thrusting balls-deep inside her as she rubbed her own clit, stimulating herself as he shot her to the heavens.

More and more erotic thoughts passed through her mind until her panties were soaked and she twisted with the need for relief.

Finally, she managed to pull up outside Gregor's lodgings. Barely remembering to lock her ancient Cruiser, she hurried up the walkway. She rang the doorbell and tried to bring some semblance of order to her hair. She had run her hands through it so many times, it looked like a giant mess.

The door opened and a large, masculine hand struck out, grabbed her, and pulled her inside. She squeaked, until she saw Gregor's dark blond hair and laughing silver eyes.

"Ooh." She tried to stay angry, but couldn't help the smile that crossed her face. "Don't scare me like that! My mind hasn't been focused at all since I entered your cubicle this morning."

Gregor laughed, released her hand, and she couldn't help herself. She rushed to him, cradled his face in her hands and kissed him deeply. She pressed her lips as tightly to his as they could manage, thrusting her tongue deep into his mouth. She wanted to drink from him until she never needed any other food or liquid again.

She pressed her breasts and damp pussy along his body, wanting to crawl inside him until she lived beneath his skin next to him. If it had been possible, she would want to be a part of him and never separate from him ever again.

Thankfully, Gregor seemed to need to touch and taste her just as much as she. Minutes ticked by as they hungrily kissed and touched, pressed and grabbed for each other. Animalistic sounds came from both of them as they caressed and tangled their tongues and hands together.

Lani felt slightly shocked at herself, she had never acted this way before, never had this burning, desperate need deep inside herself. Yet with Gregor, it all felt so right, so natural. On top of that, she simply couldn't seem to help herself. She *needed* to be as close as possible to him, much like she needed air to breathe and credits to exist.

Both of them panting heavily, Gregor finally pulled away. With one movement, he stripped his robe from him.

"You're overdressed," he said sensually, teasingly. Lani smiled and toed off her shoes. With quick, concise movements she pulled her work suit from her body. Nearly tearing her panties in her rush to strip, she finally stood free of them, gloriously naked, her skin hot and prickling with need.

She felt herself grow even damper, her entire body began to ache with the need to wrap itself around her man as he slowly let himself look at her up and down. Lani smiled sexily, and squashed the urge to preen in front of him.

Gregor slowly came to her, held her arms steady as he kissed her and walked them both backward. "My room," was all he could get out between hungry, biting kisses.

Lani nodded, not even wanting to move her mouth long enough to verbalize her response. She could feel the difference in temperature when they entered his room. Here it was warmer, more comfortable. The temperature definitely a few degrees higher. Skin being naked for long periods of time would not be a problem in this climate.

Gregor kept on walking her backward until Lani came to the solid mass of the bed against the back of her legs. With a gentle shove, he pushed her down and then promptly fell on top of her. She laughed as he put all his weight on his hands and knees.

"I thought you would squash me," she laughed, twining her arms around his neck and trying to draw him back down toward her body.

"Never," he insisted as he bent down to kiss her again. Lani spread her legs eagerly, damp with the waiting. She moaned and arched her back as Gregor merely rubbed his hot tip against the apex of her thighs and didn't plunge into her as she craved.

With a final, fierce kiss, Gregor stood up and opened a drawer. He withdrew a tube of body lube. He nodded his head toward the top of the bed.

"Hold on, darling, my patience is about to crack."

Lani rolled over and crawled up on all fours to hold on to the headboard. She found it amazing that with practically no foreplay, she literally had flooded with desire to have him.

Lani jerked slightly back as soft leather restraints were clasped around her wrists, locking her hands to the headboard of Gregor's bed. She turned slightly, looked back to him.

"It's been a part of my fantasy for too long," he insisted with a sexy smile. She carefully looked over his shaggy dark blond hair, saw the love and desire melting inside his liquid silver eyes.

Lani gulped, her voice hoarse and scratchy, she could only manage to say, "Me, too," before she watched him move back to the drawers. When he removed a thin scarf, she felt her heart accelerate.

The way in which it shimmered in the dim light, she knew it was made from the finest *brackka*-silk. Ruinously expensive, but a favorite instrument for the bondage crowd. During her research, she had discovered that in certain lights, the silk would let one see through it, yet in other lights, it was the best of blindfolds. Lani squirmed as she though of other uses, much further down the track with which she and Gregor could play with the scarf.

"I want your senses heightened, little girl," he purred into her ear as he tied the deliciously soft scarf across her eyes. "Much as I pride myself on giving my partners as much pleasure as they can stand, I have wanted you for too long, need you too much. I have a feeling this first time will be fast, rough and utterly delicious for the both of us. With your sight gone, the sensations I can give you will only heighten the arousal I can bring between us both."

Lani shivered in undeniable lust his words invoked in her. She supposed her fantasies of the last two weeks and the rather vivid thoughts all throughout the entire day might have something to do with it, but she still shivered in lust as she continued to imagine just what Gregor could do to her.

More than that, she knew with a startling clarity *just* how much she trusted Gregor. No one else, in her entire life, had been allowed to bind her, to blindfold her. She obviously loved and trusted the man more than anyone she had any other man or lover throughout her life.

Lani could hear, clear as day, the sound of a tube being opened, she could hear Gregor's ragged breathing as he obviously tried to rein in some control over himself.

She decided to tease him more. "Gregor," she said huskily, enjoying the chance to play sex kitten. "I've been fantasizing about this for weeks, months. I'm so wet you could probably slide right in me and not even pause for breath."

Lani gasped as she felt the heat of Gregor's skin directly behind her. She jumped at his warm hand on her hip, and two thick fingers stroke her pussy lips, collected the juice that flowed down there.

"Darlin'," he drawled, "tonight I'm not interested in your delicious pussy. I'm more interested in...other...orifices."

Lani smiled as he finally touched the blunt, hot tip of his finger lightly against her back passage. She gasped and felt herself arch her back as he gently stroked one thick, lubed finger into her hidden passage. Blindfolded as she was, she could also hear his own ragged breathing, the rumblings deep in his throat as he finally inserted his thick finger and deeply embedded it in her ass.

Breathing deeply, she relaxed her muscles and pressed her ass out more. She could feel the heat radiating from Gregor's body as he crouched behind her, ready and desperate to be inside her. Yet even though she knew he desperately wanted to give her what she craved more than she had ever known possible, he still tried to draw out the moment, still tried to give her every drop of pleasure he could cope with.

As he stroked his finger so deeply inside her ass, tried to twist the digit slightly to stretch her walls for the penetration of his cock, Lani was amazed at how much she wanted more. Right now.

"Gregor," she pleaded, amazed to hear the rusty timbre of her own voice.

"I hear you, little girl. And I'd like to point out, as much as I want to ram my cock into you right now, I'm doing my best to stretch you."

Lani gasped again as he added a second finger deeply inside her. With the two fingers fluted and stretching her, she felt as if she were on the brink of orgasm.

"Touch my clit," she pleaded, not able to explain anything more than the burning desire raging through her. She screamed as she felt Gregor's other hand gently reach down and his fingers stroked over her clit.

She flew apart with the intensity of her orgasm, with hardly any stroking from her man. She could hear the laughter and pride in his voice as he spoke.

"Damn, you really are hot for it, aren't you, little girl?"

Lani tried to catch her breath, so she could say something, but nothing intelligent came to mind.

"Well," he continued darkly, "if you're that hot for it, then maybe you'll love this reaming as much as I love giving it."

Lani just nodded, wanting to feel the thick length of his cock slide deeply inside her. She knew she could no longer deny her fantasies, could no longer repress the darkly submissive side of her nature.

"Do it, Gregor," she said softly, knowing he could hear her.

"It will be my pleasure, Lani," he said, and she moaned as she felt him remove his two slick fingers. She couldn't help her shiver of awareness as he pressed the heavy heat of his erection against the top of her ass.

Even though he had warned her, over and over, that he would ream her, that he would give it all to her hard, and hot, and fast, still he tried to prepare her. He pressed more lube up her ass, and she could clearly hear him greasing his own cock, trying to prepare her for even more pleasure, trying to make his eventual penetration as easy for her as possible.

"Ready, baby?" was the only verbal warning he gave her as he strongly pressed his two fingers into her passage. This time he was not being gentle, though neither would Lani say he was being particularly rough.

This time, instead of gently trying to set her aflame, he was stretching her passage for the insertion of his enormous cock. Lani rolled her head back and moaned, the full, heavy feeling of his sawing fingers both slightly painful but still incredibly erotic.

She could hardly believe she wanted this so much. Even though the painfully tight stretch caused her some twinges, the erotic pulling sensation was sweet and hot.

She wanted more.

Desperately.

When his third finger joined them, she knew he would tease her a little. The pad of his fingers stroked her inner walls, making shivers rush through her body. Lani tried to let go of the headboard, wanting to finger her clit which ached to be touched, yet she was recalled when her hands couldn't move.

She smiled, she had utterly forgotten she was bound.

Lani felt her body begin to shake once again. She didn't know how much longer she could hold back her climax. This all happened so incredibly quick, she couldn't believe she was on the knife edge of reason for a second time, already.

"Gregor," she pleaded, her voice wobbly, "I need you. I'm going to come really soon."

"I hear you, darling, and I know what you mean. I wanted this to last so much longer, I wanted to tease you like you've been teasing me."

"Trust me," she breathed heavily, "if you tease me much more I'll be wrung dry."

Gregor chortled wickedly. She felt his other hand fall to her pussy, picking up the running juices.

"Baby, the last thing I want is for you to be wrung dry." Lani felt her breath catch as he spread her own juices, slicking his cock even more with them. She barely heard the rest of his sentence, so lost was she in her own world of erotic fulfillment.

"I want you pumped full," he finished.

With that, he turned her, so her ass aligned with his cock. He withdrew his fingers, slicking extra lubricant around the outside of her hole. Lani had to smile how even with him obviously on the edge. With her nearly insensate with desire, he still seemed to be trying to make this first time as easy for her as possible.

In one long, slow thrust, he penetrated her, causing her back to arch and her to moan long and deep. She could hardly believe the wealth of sensations her body catalogued for her. She found herself bombarded with a million different feelings, all at the same time.

The feeling was unlike anything she had imagined. He was thick, wide, and fiery hot. She felt utterly split, so very full it was indescribable. For a moment, they both just held there, pulsing, breathing deeply.

"My clit," she gasped, startled when he groaned, "Not yet," and began to pull himself away from her.

She felt even more sensation, if that were possible, as Gregor moved again. Slowly sawing his way out of her ravaged ass, she could have sworn he hit even more nerves, touched her on an even deeper level than he had reached on his way in. Her muscles clamped down on him, urging him to stay, but still he pulled away from her.

When just the very tip of his cock sat at her opening, they both paused again, panting, gasping for breath.

"In," she panted. "I want you inside me, Gregor."

And then he went wild. He pressed inside her as if he were storming a castle. He pressed so deeply into her she fell facedown on the bed and cried out. He came down on top of her, pressing her farther into the softness.

In and out.

In and out.

In and out he pulled over and over again. Lani knew she would never feel this way with anyone else. Gregor erased every other man until only he remained. Lani cried and moaned, screamed and shouted. She begged and pleaded and surrendered to her man completely.

Finally, she felt her pussy *and* her ass seize up and contract, over and over as the angle of his penetration pressed her clit firmly down onto the bed. She could feel Gregor inside her ass, throbbing away. He shouted and she could feel the warm stickiness of his seed pouring inside her, over and over as he shot himself deeply inside her ass.

He filled her up, and then she could feel it leaking outside of her ass and down her thighs.

Panting, he fell back down on top of her, and they lay there for a minute, panting and seeing stars.

Lani could have happily stayed there forever, never move ever again. She smiled tiredly as she felt him press a catch on the restraints and they fell behind the bed. With her hands free, she pulled the *brackka*-silk scarf from her eyes.

"That's one expensive piece of cloth," she said inanely, wanting to stretch the tender moment out a bit.

She turned to see Gregor smile at her.

"Yeah, but it's worth its weight in credits."

Slowly, he pulled out from her, a small gush of seed trickling with him. Lani moaned and moved her head to the side. Lani turned very slightly onto her side, enjoying the slight twinge in her ass. She watched silently while Gregor pulled a damp washercloth from the table resting beside the bed. He cleaned himself, and then carefully, almost reverently turned her so he could cleanse her as well.

When he had finished, he replaced the cloth and snuggled down beside her on the bed. Lani reached out her hand and grabbed Gregor's arm. He came around to her front and pulled her close to him.

"That was amazing," she said softly, drinking in his features. He seemed so much happier, more serene, after this bout of lovemaking. It looked like he were the most content man in the entire galaxy.

She had to smile as he gently stroked her face with his finger.

"Amazing enough that you will Bond with me? You know we're destined to be together forever. Why not merge yourself truly with me?"

Lani smiled. In her heart, she knew she wanted to Bond with this man, and none other, but that didn't mean she had to make it easy for him. "We've hardly known each other a month," she pointed out with a smile.

She nearly laughed as Gregor arrogantly raised an eyebrow. "And you think this makes a difference?"

She did laugh to that. "Okay, so we know each other better than most friends of fifty years. But you have to admit, this is all a bit sudden, and we haven't exactly learned the small things about each other. Can we wait a bit? See what we both want to do with our lives? I want to watch over Leif until he's finished his training with the Guild, and I wouldn't mind exploring the galaxy a little."

Gregor hushed her and kissed her softly, lovingly. "Just stay with me for now. We can discuss everything else later. I'd love to see the galaxy *with* you. We can do all these things together. Besides, I rather liked the idea of convincing you night and day to Bond with me."

Lani smiled at that and looked up into his eyes. "You know. I rather like that idea myself. How about we just let it ride for a short while?"

She laughed as Gregor turned her onto her stomach. When he pressed his body along hers, covering her with his heat, she wriggled teasingly.

When his hand came down to stroke her labia, she moaned.

"How about I try to convince you?" he whispered enticingly in her ear, his breath hot against her neck.

"That could work," she gasped softly.

As he slowly stroked his already firm cock into her, he nibbled on her neck, and then lifted his face.

"Lani," he whispered into her ear. He sounded like every erotic dream she had ever had.

"What?" she gasped, trying to keep herself from coming once again.

"Bond with me," he whispered to her.

Lani groaned. With his cock sliding in and out of her, with his hand at her clit and his dark promises being made in her ear, she knew she was lost.

"Yes," she panted, canting her hips up to give him a deeper access. "Yes!" she said louder, desperately needing him to stroke into her harder.

She could feel his smile against her shoulder as he gently bit her, the small amount of pain exquisitely blending with the rush of pleasure his cock gave her. Lani seized up and flew over the edge of her climax. She screamed as she came, and Gregor was only a step behind her.

He pumped into her, over and over, and within moments they were both at rest once more, snuggled together spoon fashion.

"I knew I could convince you," he said smugly, in the way she suspected men across the galaxy had.

"Yeah," she murmured sleepily, "but I'm sure to get you back sometime."

She snuggled deeper into his embrace as Gregor nuzzled her neck.

"Undoubtedly," he agreed. And Lani slowly fell into a peaceful, settled sleep in her future Bondmate's arms.

Enjoy an excerpt from:
TAILSPIN

Mirry slid his palm from her shoulder to her hand, lingering over the caress. He grasped it and drew it up slowly, over his knee. Higher.

"You may as well look, you know. It won't go away while you're touching me." His voice was so absolutely toneless, she knew he must be amused by her naivety. But when she glanced into his face, there was nothing to be seen but calm and concentration.

Nonetheless, the suspicion he was laughing at her lingered and the sting of it gave her courage.

She let herself look.

And made a startling discovery. "Lufra! There's no hair on your body."

"Only feathers," he agreed. "Except on my head."

Something tugged her closer and she realized his tail was snugged around her waist, the feathered end of it brushing her belly. But that was a peripheral consideration. She leaned forward, enthralled, and his hips rose slightly off the bed.

She'd never cared much for testicles, though Veryl had been inordinately proud of his. They'd been big enough for manliness, she supposed—she had no grounds for comparison. But they'd been wrinkled and hairy and pendulous, not round and rosy-gold and tight like ripe gaeta fruits on the vine. Bare and smooth.

All the air in the wagon evaporated. She couldn't suck enough of it into her lungs.

When she licked her lips, Mirry made a purring noise deep in his throat. His…his… Lufra, she had to brace herself to form the word, even in her head. His *cock* reared over his ridged stomach, a golden column. The broad head flushed a deep amber and a pearl of moisture glimmered on the tip, gilded by the light of the lantern. As she watched, he took it in one hand, running his thumb over the satiny skin with casual competence. His chest rose and fell, the gilded nipples fiercely erect.

Shameless, he was absolutely shameless.

"True enough." He chuckled and her sex contracted with greed at the wicked, masculine sound. Gods, she'd spoken aloud! Either that or he'd read her mind.

"Fledge." Plumage rustled as he tilted his head, holding her pinned with the intensity of his raptor's gaze. Suddenly, she had an insight into the mortal terrors of small tasty creatures like bunrats. "Touch me."

There was no room for choice in his tone, nothing but imperious demand. Fledge froze, immobilized by longing, paralyzed by fear.

The seconds stretched. Finally, Mirry sighed. The strange, tufted brows drew together. He lifted his fingers away from hers, uncoiled his tail from around her waist. Without the warmth of his flesh, a chill slithered down her spine.

He tucked his hands behind his head, revealing more russet-colored, wispy down, this time in the hollows under his arms. The sight affected her strangely, made her chest hurt.

"Please," he said. The word seemed dragged out of him. Even as his hips lifted and his cock quivered, his sculptured lips compressed in a thin line of displeasure. Fledge knew that expression. She'd angered him. Gods. Her spine stiffened while her stomach roiled. Imperceptibly, she withdrew and Mirry sighed. The silence stretched, but he made no further move toward her and finally, she was able to raise her eyes to his.

She drowned in the topaz depths. "I'll never see you again," she husked. "I know that."

"Perhaps." He shrugged and feathers whispered across her pillows. "Perhaps not."

The moment he'd set her free, perversely, she wanted to be held. She shook her head, amazed at herself. Her brain must be disordered by such unadulterated beauty. He'd hypnotized her.

"No?" He squeezed his eyes shut and inhaled deeply. A muscle at the corner of his jaw knotted. "Ah well, I'll not force you." He sat up with a wince, a tawny angel shining in her shabby wagon. "I'd better go."

"No! You can't! I mean—" She swallowed, conscious her voice had risen to an undignified squeak. "Your wings. I have to— They're still filthy and your wound…"

"Don't worry, little Fledge." He trailed his knuckles across her cheek. "I'll be fine."

He was really going. Really. Forever. All sense left her. The seconds tiptoed by, rich with the strange and varied noises of the Ten Nations Fair at night. A man whistled tunelessly in the distance. Harness jingled in a cheerful counterpoint, one of the vranee whickered.

"You could close your eyes," she whispered.

In the warmth and the lamplight, the silence seemed endless. A night wind swept over the campground, making canvas flap and timber creak. The little wagon rocked the slightest bit.

Finally, Mirry said, "So I could." Every movement graceful and deliberate, he took the bowl from her nerveless fingers and laid it on the floor. Then he lay back against the pillows, reached out a long arm and drew her down to his chest. He tipped up her chin with one hand, tilted his head and fitted his mouth over hers.

Her first gasp was one of surprise, her second a moan of pleasure. Ah Goddess, he kissed as though time was an irrelevance, nibbling lightly at her lower lip, running his tongue gently over the curve of it. There was no rush, no slobbering or pushing, just an ocean of gentle delight, of satin smooth and tingling texture, wet and hot and firm. As it went on and on and he showed no sign of impatience or dissatisfaction, Fledge allowed herself to relax, to sink into the intoxicating depths of it, a fraction at a time.

Mirry still held her hand in his, his long fingers laced through hers. When the other flailed about, he caught it and skimmed it over the good side of his chest, brushing her palm over the fine feathers. They were soft and cool, tickling her skin, the way she imagined the breast of a bird might do. But underneath was a wealth of smooth, warm solidity.

Shyly, she let her tongue creep out and play with his. Mirry made a humming sound of approval and drew her closer, spearing his fingers into her hair and dislodging the tie she used to keep the curls from swinging in her face. He deepened the kiss, luring her on until she was so lost in sensation, she would have crawled right inside his skin if she'd been able. His elegant fingers cradled the back of her skull, his big body was hard and furnace hot beneath hers and his tail clamped around her waist, a girdle of silk-clad muscle. Simultaneously ravished and comforted, Fledge moaned into his mouth.

He took his time, but finally, infinitely slowly, he let her surface, brushing his lips across hers, kissing her eyelids, the tip of her nose, laying a trail of nibbles along her jaw. Under her clutching fingers, his shoulders were rigid, as hard as marble, belying the tenderness of his lips. At last, he pulled back to stare into her face.

For an instant, surprise swam in his eyes, but before she could work out why that might be so, he smiled and Fledge lost her mind. It was a grin of unabashed boyish delight and it lit his face with an unholy beauty. Reeling under the impact, she gurgled, as stunned as if he'd hit her with his fist.

"Sweet," he murmured. "So pouty and soft. Like a little cushion." He rested the flat of his thumb on the center of her lower lip. "Just here." His voice dropped a register. "Gods, the things I could do with your mouth…"

Enjoy an excerpt from:
SPIRITS SHARED

Copyright © JORY STRONG, 2007.
All Rights Reserved, Ellora's Cave Publishing, Inc.

Clay's heart ached. Guilt shredded his guts. He hadn't been with another man or another woman since he'd stumbled into a bookstore and fallen head over heels in love—or at least deeply in lust—with the soft-spoken blonde who was reading a book to a group of kids in the children's section.

They'd meshed right from the start and he'd known that Jess was the one he wanted to share his life with. He loved her. Period. End of story.

You wish it were the end of the story.

Clay stabbed a fry into a pool of catsup. He fought the fear that had been threatening to suffocate him since "coming out" while he was driving. Christ! How stupid had that been?

He glanced up from his plate to find her looking out the window again. It hurt to see her like this. It'd kill him if she started crying.

His eyes went to the ring on her finger. At least she hadn't hurtled it back at him. She hadn't screamed or cursed or called him names. Not that he would have blamed her, though if she had he probably would have wrecked the car.

Her looks might have caught his attention in the first place but it was everything else about her, especially her innate gentleness, that had completely hooked him. She could take care of herself but he found he *liked* taking care of her. She could be tough when she needed to be, but she wasn't afraid to be utterly feminine with him.

Fuck. Maybe they could settle this in bed. Maybe he should find out if there was a hotel in this seven-building town and take Jessica there. He could reassure her with his body that he loved and desired her. Hell, not just loved and desired, but desperately needed her in his life.

Clay rubbed his chest in an effort to erase some of the tightness there. Christ, *need* was too tame a word, especially when it came to sex with Jessica.

He craved it like an addict who was always looking for the next fix. He could be whitewater rafting on rough water and he'd still get hard just thinking about the way she yielded and went submissive when he required that from her. Fuck, more than once when he'd been rock climbing he'd gotten a boner he could have used as a chisel when his mind had strayed to how she'd accepted the rougher aspects of his sexuality — not that he'd ever, ever hurt her.

Yeah right, asshole. Look at her and tell yourself she's one happy camper at the moment.

Clay risked another glance and wished he knew what she was thinking. What a fucking mess. They'd been engaged for three months. They'd dated for nine before that. He'd have proposed on the first date, that's how sure he was that she was the right *woman* for him. But she was more cautious by nature, a little less quick to grab for the brass ring than he was, so he'd taken the time she needed.

In retrospect he realized he'd also been testing himself. By the time he'd finally popped the question he'd convinced himself that he was mainly hetero. Yeah, he noticed guys and sometimes he fantasized, but mostly he wanted to fuck Jess.

The last group trip he'd led ripped that false sense of security away like it was toilet paper. He'd been tempted, tempted to the point where only his old ironclad rule to never get involved with paying clients or client employees had kept him from doing something stupid.

Clay's heart thundered in his chest just thinking about how close he'd come on his last trip to trashing any hope for a future with Jess. If he betrayed her with either a man or a woman, she would never forgive him. He'd be out of her life permanently.

It'd been a wake-up call, not just for the present but for the future. He broke into a cold sweat whenever he imagined what might happen down the road. It was easy to envision a situation where she was home with their kids and he was on a trip where there were guys who weren't clients. It would happen in a weak moment, maybe after the rush of conquering some span of water or mountain or maybe just because he'd gone years without being with another man.

Christ, he would lose everything that mattered to him. Everything. Her. Their kids. His self-respect. Everything.

It'd be easy if he could see a shrink and get "cured" or take a pill and bingo, no more urge for gay sex. For Jess, he'd do either of those things—he'd give up an inherent part of himself. But one, those options weren't available. And two, she'd never ask it of him anyway.

He knew Jessica had no problem with someone being gay or bi. Hell, that's what had led to his confession in the car.

He'd intended to wait until they'd gotten to the cabin and settled in for the week. He'd imagined himself telling her after they'd made love in front of a roaring fire. But then she'd started talking to him about a book she was thinking of writing, a teen "coming out" book and *he'd* come out. Christ. Seeing her hurt was tearing him up. Somehow he had to convince her they could work this out.

He didn't want an open marriage where they both screwed around like they were dogs with an itch that could be scratched by anyone. It'd kill him to be with her and wonder if she'd been with someone else earlier.

There'd been a time in his life when he'd been quick to fuck anyone who caught his eye. But even before he'd met Jess, he'd slowed down on the casual sex. Not that he'd been a saint, but deep down he was already waiting for the right person—the right woman. He'd never pictured himself setting up house with another guy. He'd never thought much about what it would mean to be bi and married.

The truth was, he'd never been one to overplan the future. Yeah, he was meticulous about the adventure trips because lives were on the line. But when it came to the big picture of his personal life he trusted that he'd see the brass ring and be ready to grab it when it came along.

He'd seen Jessica and he'd known she was the one. Now he had to hang on to her. The trouble was, the only way he could see that happening was if they were a threesome instead of a twosome.

Why an electronic book?

We live in the Information Age — an exciting time in the history of human civilization, in which technology rules supreme and continues to progress in leaps and bounds every minute of every day. For a multitude of reasons, more and more avid literary fans are opting to purchase e-books instead of paper books. The question from those not yet initiated into the world of electronic reading is simply: *Why?*

1. *Price.* An electronic title at Ellora's Cave Publishing and Cerridwen Press runs anywhere from 40% to 75% less than the cover price of the exact same title in paperback format. Why? Basic mathematics and cost. It is less expensive to publish an e-book (no paper and printing, no warehousing and shipping) than it is to publish a paperback, so the savings are passed along to the consumer.

2. *Space.* Running out of room in your house for your books? That is one worry you will never have with electronic books. For a low one-time cost, you can purchase a handheld device specifically designed for e-reading. Many e-readers have large, convenient screens for viewing. Better yet, hundreds of titles can be stored within your new library — on a single microchip. There are a variety of e-readers from different manufacturers. You can also read e-books on your PC or laptop computer. (Please note that Ellora's Cave does not endorse any specific brands.

You can check our websites at www.ellorascave.com or www.cerridwenpress.com for information we make available to new consumers.)

3. *Mobility.* Because your new e-library consists of only a microchip within a small, easily transportable e-reader, your entire cache of books can be taken with you wherever you go.

4. *Personal Viewing Preferences.* Are the words you are currently reading too small? Too large? Too... ANNOYING? Paperback books cannot be modified according to personal preferences, but e-books can.

5. *Instant Gratification.* Is it the middle of the night and all the bookstores near you are closed? Are you tired of waiting days, sometimes weeks, for bookstores to ship the novels you bought? Ellora's Cave Publishing sells instantaneous downloads twenty-four hours a day, seven days a week, every day of the year. Our webstore is never closed. Our e-book delivery system is 100% automated, meaning your order is filled as soon as you pay for it.

Those are a few of the top reasons why electronic books are replacing paperbacks for many avid readers.

As always, Ellora's Cave and Cerridwen Press welcome your questions and comments. We invite you to email us at Comments@ellorascave.com or write to us directly at Ellora's Cave Publishing Inc., 1056 Home Avenue, Akron, OH 44310-3502.

THE
⚚ ELLORA'S CAVE ⚚
LIBRARY

Stay up to date with Ellora's Cave Titles in
Print with our Quarterly Catalog.

erridwen, the Celtic Goddess of wisdom, was the muse who brought inspiration to story-tellers and those in the creative arts. Cerridwen Press encompasses the best and most innovative stories in all genres of today's fiction. Visit our site and discover the newest titles by talented authors who still get inspired - much like the ancient storytellers did, once upon a time.

CERRIDWEN PRESS

www.cerridwenpress.com

Discover for yourself why readers can't get enough
of the multiple award-winning publisher
Ellora's Cave.

Whether you prefer e-books or paperbacks,

be sure to visit EC on the web at
www.ellorascave.com

for an erotic reading experience that will leave you
breathless.

LaVergne, TN USA
04 April 2011
222767LV00001B/154/P